Stephen Paul knows horses. Stephen Paul knows how to write suspense. Put the two together, and the result is a gripping western thriller with a plot more twisted than a desert rattler that will keep you guessing till the very end.

—Karen Dionne, author, *Whisper of the Cat*

                 *   *   *   *   *   *   *   *   *

Stephen Paul, an exciting new writer, has captured the heart-tugging drama of man's greed versus wild horses, juxtaposed over what some still refer to as one of the last frontiers - rugged and raw Wyoming. It is interesting how Stephen Paul has woven this tapestry of animal and man with the ever present shadows of the unique Wyoming culture. The story takes place in a setting where treacherous weather, wild horses and true surroundings found on the prairies of the Eastern Rocky Mountains provide what will hopefully be a rich visual Hollywood Film one day.

As a film producer, I read Stephen Paul's, *Can Horses Cry*, with the eye of a visual adventurer who enters an untamed land with untamed elements that seem to be caught in the time warp of the Wyoming culture. It was fascinating to read about such a raw environment, complete with indigenous logic in contrast with what we in Los Angeles construe as the norm. Today's Wyoming, its horses, its people, and its weather provide a vestige of Wyoming reality slowly eroding. Visual, raw and dramatic........*Can Horses Cry*!

—Larry Wilcox, actor and star of the hit TV series CHiPs, and producer for the past 30 years on several shows including Lassie, CHiPs and the Ray Bradbury Theater.

CAN HORSES CRY?

By Stephen Paul

Can Horses Cry?

Stephen Paul

Published by

Sky Ray Publishing
3000 Tuttle Creek Blvd #42
Manhattan, KS 66505-7122

http://www.skyraypublishing.com

Printed in the United States of America

This book is dedicated to my wife and soulmate, Judy, who's patience and editing made this book possible. Also, my father, Robert, and my two children, Brian and Melanie.

A special thanks goes to Jim Connelly of Denver, Co, for the hours on the telephone we spent discussing what I'd written and his blunt suggestions when he thought I went awry.

I would like to acknowledge the following people for their encouragement and support of my writing:

Circuit Court Judge, Wade Waldrip, Ginger Fisher and Susan Harberts – their enthusiasm made me want to write more; Linda Connelly, Ron and Becky Fields, Nicki Epp, Terry Walcker, Dave Christman, Lawrence Martinez, Jerrilyn Schulze, Paul Fritz., Blaine Wood and my British, cyber buddy author, Simon Watson. Author Karen Dionne has given me invaluable help with the informative side of the pre-publishing process and the support and help from the Redrumtavern writers group I belong to has been unsurpassed.

I especially want to thank Ray Clotfelter, executive publisher of Sky Ray Publishing, for his willingness to take a chance on a new author.

And last, but not least, the buckskin stallion roaming the prairie and foothills of Green Mountain, leading his herd of wild horses..

Stephen Paul
October 20, 2003
Rawlins, Wyoming

Prologue

The stallion heard something. Lifting his head he turned toward the canyon ridge to the west. The rest of the herd sensed something in the air but waited for the stallion to lead them. Marred with scars from battles he'd fought, the buckskin quivered with anticipation and fear, not knowing what challenge was coming. He pawed the ground anxiously then started trotting around the herd, gathering them up to make a run.

Suddenly, shots rang out! Echoing in the crisp day where five shots sounded like fifty, the horses, confused and panicked, started breaking away in a dead run. Some dropped as they were shot; others ran into the older, slower, horses. Mares and colts, screaming with pain from the bullets, fell as if their feet were ripped out from under them. Some were dead when they hit the ground; many thrashed and squealed as they were crippled from the assault. Then it was over. The dust and gun smoke still lingered in the air and the ground looked as if a hailstorm had rained down blood rather than pellets of ice.

The stallion and the remainder of his herd were still running to safety, blinded by fear and the smell of death.

Chapter One

When his eyes opened they were blinded by the sharp light streaming in between the window blinds. His lips were stuck together from the drool that had pooled by his head, and a harsh headache made his eyes throb with every beat of his heart.

Although he had no memory of how many beers he had drunk the night before, the queasiness in his stomach let him know it was enough that he would probably have to throw up.

A shaky hand threw the covers back and he staggered out of bed. The empty side of the bed told him his wife had slept in the guest room again. When he looked in the mirror over the sink, bloodshot eyes stared back at him from a haggard and drawn face. Brown hair, graying on the sides, stood out in stringy tufts and reflected an image of being electrocuted and some-how surviving.

"Oh Christ, here we go." He took a deep breath knowing what was coming, yet having to do it. The finger went down his throat until the gagging started, then he leaned over the toilet and brought up what was left in his stomach. The retching covered the sound of Dana's approach.

"That's just great, Bailey." His wife was leaning on the bathroom doorway, frowning at him. "Jesus, you're forty-nine years old and still drinking so much it makes you puke. What's wrong with this picture?"

The toilet paper he had wiped his mouth with stuck to his unshaven face. "Shut up, Dana," his voice croaked, "I don't feel like hearing a sermon right now."

"What the hell has happened to you? You're not the same guy who was here six months ago. *I'm* not calling you in sick if you don't go to work, so you better hurry or you'll be late." She turned away before he could say anything and went to the back bathroom, slamming the door behind her.

He pissed for what seemed like ten minutes. *Christ, this day's starting off good.* Bailey climbed in the shower holding his sour belly. With the water on, he turned the hot off and almost yelled when the cold water hit him. His hand clutched the shower water control and turned it to cycle back and forth. Hot-cold-hot. After getting out, the full-length mirror showed an image he didn't like. *What the hell am I doing? I'm acting like a damn teenager.* He brushed his teeth and tongue, shaved, then dressed in his uniform, slightly wrinkled from the day before. *I oughta change, but the hell with it.* The Pepto-Bismol beckoned to him from the medicine cabinet. He drank a quarter of the bottle and left for work.

Bailey walked into the Bureau of Land Management building and opened the door to his office. The stenciling on the glass read, "Bailey Calhoun, Regional Area Investigator."

His job consisted of investigating the theft of property from BLM land, lease infringement and most crimes that violated the laws governing lands cared for by the BLM. He carried a gun more due to tradition than necessity, though at different times he had shot some rattlesnakes.

After five years working at the local police department, Bailey had quit when his supervisors didn't accept his personal view of justice versus the letter of the law. Justice took precedence over the law; *that* was his belief. Bailey decided working at the Bureau of Land Management would be a better career move.

Before joining the police department, Bailey had been in the Marines less than five months when he had been hit in the back by shrapnel from a hand grenade. Bailey Calhoun, just a few years past his teens, had caught the tail end of Vietnam and it had reached up and bitten him.

Chapter Two

Fred Rysdon was holding a newspaper as he walked into Bailey's office. "What do you think about those wild horses killed over in the Red Desert?" Rysdon was a BLM surveyor who was forty years old, short, nearly bald and portly. Everyone heard how Rysdon wanted to be an investigator and knew it never would happen. But in his eyes, the investigation division was nearly equal in stature with the FBI.

"I haven't seen the paper yet, Fred. What are you talking about?" Bailey hoped his eyes had turned their normal blue.

Putting on his reading glasses, Rysdon read from the paper.

"Says here someone called into the Sweetwater County Sheriff's Office about some dead horses. They found twenty-three wild horses shot and killed down in a small canyon. Figured it was an entire herd and they'd been dead around a week. The Sheriff's Office reports they don't have a motive or any suspects, investigation continuing."

"That's about par for the course," Bailey said. "Some crazy assholes getting their kicks. Christ, that pisses me off."

Bailey had been accused of having more compassion for animals than he did for people. When he was a senior in high school, he had beaten the crap out of a man who was whipping a dog with a wide leather belt and a huge buckle. Bailey had knocked him down and beat him with the same belt. If the cops hadn't liked Bailey and talked the man out of pressing charges, Bailey would have been charged with assault. Fortunately, the guy was on parole and decided not to make an issue out of it.

"I need to ask Williams if any dead horses have been reported around here, particularly the refuge." He told Ryson.

"It seems like when a story about killing horses or something like that hits the papers, somebody else wants to try the same thing. The stupid bastards think they'll become famous. I'd ask Travis but I doubt if he'd have heard anything, and if he did, he'd have forgotten already." He popped a couple of aspirins.

"My ears will be open, Bailey." Fred lowered his glasses and put the newspaper on the desk. "If I hear or see anything, you'll be the first one to know, and if you need any help, I'll be around." He left Bailey sitting in his chair looking at the article.

Why the hell did Dennis have to go and have a damn heart attack?

Besides the booze, a big part of Bailey's problem was being moved into the administrative side of the job. He was to take over Dennis Cummings's job when Dennis retired, which was coming up in two months.

"Dennis," Bailey would say, "you're the best boss I've worked for, don't go. Stay until you reach the magic mark of seventy-five years old."

Dennis was the Assistant Regional Supervisor, a job he had transferred into from Las Vegas when Bailey turned it down five years ago. Bailey wanted to stay out in the field, where he felt he belonged, not in some lousy office all day, shuffling papers. If Bailey could hold on, he could retire in six years.

With Dennis undergoing open-heart surgery three weeks ago, he would remain out on sick leave, then take retirement. John Williams, the supervisor who had come from the same Las Vegas district as Cummings two years ago, told Bailey he had no choice. Williams expected Bailey to stay in the office and learn the job, then be prepared to take it over officially on July first.

"Dammit! I don't want the job." Bailey had yelled.

"I don't want you to have it either, Calhoun. If I could do it, I'd get someone out of the district who has a hell of a lot better attitude than you do." Williams shouted back.

Bailey had felt his face flush. "Let's settle this now. Call the district headquarters, I don't want to be in administration. Christ, my entire career has been in the field. I'm good at it."

"It was District that made the decision to promote you," Williams sighed. "They feel if there's someone here with twenty years experience and your background, we should promote from within." A sly smile crept upon Williams's face. "You could quit, you know. However, you might have a hard time finding another career at your age."

Calhoun was going to be the next assistant supervisor or be gone. At his age, security had a tight grip on his balls.

*   *   *   *   *   *   *   *   *

When Bailey got home after work, he found the house empty. Dana was usually home by three o'clock; she was the assistant librarian at the local library and was able to set her own hours so she normally took the early afternoons off.

Aw, shit. Don't tell me.

He went in the bedroom and saw the closet door open. Most of her clothes were gone as well as the two suitcases they kept on the floor of the closet.

With a wry grimace, he grabbed a beer from the fridge and saw an envelope with his name neatly printed in the center lying on the kitchen table. He had an idea what was in it; he took a big swallow of beer while he debated on opening the envelope.

Bailey finished the can and got himself another beer. He pulled a chair out and sitting down, opened the envelope and took the letter out.

Bailey, your first thought will be to think I'm such a coward to write you a letter rather than discuss this in person. I can't bear to watch you continuing to drag yourself down. You have a drinking problem and some demons <u>you</u> have to work out, since you won't talk or let me help. I'm going to stay

15

with Jenny for awhile to try and decide what I'm going to do. I still love you, but you're eroding my love by your actions. Please don't call me. I'll call you when I'm ready to talk. Get some help, Bailey, if you feel we still have something left and before it's too late. Love, Dana

He crumpled the letter up and threw it into the trashcan.

Christ, I know I've been drinking a little too much, but this? What other problems are coming besides my wife leaving me, getting old and having to change jobs?

He went to the couch in the living room and sat down to read the paper.

The ringing phone woke him up.

"Yeah, Calhoun." His eyes looked at the six empty beer cans on the table and he absently shook his head.

"Bailey, this is Carl. Say, I was flying over the refuge today and thought I saw something ya might be interested in. Something didn't look right down there. Something a little screwy."

"Carl, you saw something a little screwy? Can you elaborate a bit?"

"A little pissy, are ya, Bailey? I think I saw a lot of dead horses in the little canyon north of the old stage stop."

"What makes you think they were dead?" Bailey carried the phone over to the fridge and got another beer.

"It was too windy to get real low, but I banked as close as I could and it looked like a bunch of horses down. If they wasn't dead, they was sleepin'. Anyway, I thought maybe you'd want to know, but maybe ya don't." He sounded a little miffed.

"Yeah, thanks, Carl. Sorry, I was sleeping when you called, that's why I sounded so cranky."

"If I had known you was asleep at eight o'clock, I'd never have telephoned."

"Hey, no. I appreciate it. I'll check into it tomorrow and let you know what I find. Thanks, Carl, and sorry about being so shitty."

"Don't worry about it none, I heard ya been having a tough time with things."

Bailey hung up, astounded his apparent troubles were known to people around town. With Dana gone, fodder would be added to the rumor mills. Under the circumstances he figured some luck was still with him since he continued to make it to work after getting hammered so many times. It didn't take much reflection to see the fucking booze was getting a grip on him.

When he woke up the next morning he felt like crap, but not quite as bad as the morning before. When he got to his office he saw Travis Knight hanging around Williams's secretary, having coffee and telling her a story.

When Williams had hired Travis, it had been a bone of contention with Bailey. Travis was the son of Calvin Knight, who owned The Golden Eagle Gas and Exploration Company, also known as The Golden Dick; because he seemed to get everything he wanted and didn't give much back. Bailey always thought Knight had used his influence to get his kid hired; now he was being groomed to take Bailey's job.

"Hey, Travis. Come on in for a minute." Bailey threw some breath mints into his mouth as Travis came in and sat down.

"What's up, Bailey?" Travis placed his coffee cup down on some papers lying on the desk.

"Dammit, Travis. Get your cup off those papers. Shit, you've left a ring on the damn things." Bailey picked the papers up and scowled at them. "Hell, now I gotta redo these stinking reports."

"Sorry, man. What'd you want? I got some things to do."

"You been out to the refuge in the last couple of days?"

"Yeah, just yesterday. Why?"

"I had a report of some dead horses. You see them?" Bailey was watching Travis's eyes and saw them flinch.

"I found a bunch dead from winterkill, looked like. They were down inside a little canyon, the one with the road going up to the top. I was going to write the report today."

17

"What do you consider a bunch? Two horses——fifty?"

"Well...maybe a little over a dozen." Travis slipped down in the chair a bit.

"Over a dozen! Jesus Christ, Travis!"

"Look, Bailey, they were stranded in the canyon this winter and died from starvation."

"You checked them though? You're satisfied it was from winterkill?" He thought Travis wasn't telling everything in the way he averted Bailey's eyes.

"Yeah, I'm sure. I'll write the report on it today."

"Let me see it when you're finished." Bailey said.

"Sure, no problem." Travis got up and went to his desk, looking over his shoulder at Bailey once as he sat down.

Bailey walked over to Travis and leaned down, "Did you see a buckskin stallion with them?"

"I didn't see any buckskin, Bailey. Just some mares and colts, no stallions." Travis had his nose in the report he was filling out.

Bailey stretched, sucking in the extra 20 pounds on his six foot three frame. *Shit, if I could get down to 210, I'd be happy.* He liked the way Travis carried himself. At twenty-nine, Travis was trim, he was what the older generation called a flat belly. He also had collar-length blond hair. Bailey kept his hair above the ear, not quite having the guts to let it grow long, though he'd like to have tried someday. He waited to see if Travis had anything else to say.

"Something else you need, Bailey?" Travis still didn't raise his head.

"Nope, let me see the report when you're done." He went back to his office and released his stomach muscles. *I can't believe how a few years can change a man's body.* The schedule planner didn't have many entries in it for the day. If he could just have an easy day, maybe things would look a little brighter later. He reread the article in the newspaper for the third time.

"Goddammit, Dana, what's happening to us?" The newspaper bounced off the desk, scattering pages onto the floor. A picture of a smiling Dana, standing on the bluff of Wild Horse Lookup, sat on the desktop. His eyes stayed on the picture as if an answer would come from it.

No one, except Bailey, seemed to notice the smothering feeling of despair and foreboding that surrounded him. His shoulders hunched from reflex. *Something bad is coming. I wonder what?*

Chapter Three

As the last of the gunshots echoed away, the three men got up from the ground.

"Not bad, considering the bastards started running." Streck's piercing black eyes looked at Lynch and Gomez as he smiled.

"Give me the rifles, then pick the brass up." The words came out with authority; Streck was used to being obeyed. Streck took the AR-15s and wrapped them in several towels, then lovingly put them under the back seat of the truck.

"A man's gotta take care of his tools," he told the other two men.

The AR-15s were the civilian version of the M-16. These had wire fold-up stocks and twenty-round magazines. The bullet size was .223 caliber and when the gun was fired, the bullet flew in a rocking motion, so when it hit, it tumbled. Very devastating.

Lynch and Gomez glanced at each other as they started picking up the shell casings.

"This dude's crazier than I thought." Lynch whispered to Gomez, who nodded his head. After a couple of minutes, Lynch straightened up. "We've picked up enough. I ain't no janitor."

"Yeah, me either. I can't believe Streck had us wipe out a herd of fuckin' horses. Now he's acting like he just took his dog for a walk," Gomez said.

Streck hadn't shown any emotion. He'd told them the job might include some killing, which was no problem if the price was right, but they thought he meant people. Neither Lynch nor Gomez was faint-hearted; their rap sheets showed they'd committed crimes against people. Both had previously been residents of the Colorado State Penitentiary in Canyon City. Lynch and Gomez were suspected of some violent crimes, but no one could ever prove it.

When they met Streck in the joint, he was one of the few inmates not bothered or harassed by the other cons. There was a story told several times of a tough con, a lieutenant in the Black Fist gang, who tried to make Streck his punk when Streck first came into the pen. Streck was taking a shower when Wallis, the lieutenant of the gang, went in and barred the door with a broom handle.

 Several minutes passed before the door opened. Streck was clenching his hands as he walked out, a bruise on his cheek.

"Jesus Christ." A voice whispered. Several men went into the shower area and found Wallis dead. Brutally beaten, lying in the corner of the shower with his nuts cut off and placed in his outstretched hand.

No one squealed and the administration wasn't able to prove Streck was involved. Nobody screwed with Streck after the incident. Most avoided him.

A short time later, Streck had a tattoo put on the side of his neck with a similar look to a hand holding a knife, making a slicing motion.

He was six-foot one and looked like a linebacker for the Kansas City Chiefs. He was quiet, spoke in a soft voice and kept to himself. Streck was also a psychopathic killer.

He had been on trial for attempted murder. The DA started hearing a rumor floating around saying Streck was connected to the mob in an unofficial manner, like a sub-contractor. When the main witness disappeared and the District Attorney started having problems with the other witnesses refusing to testify, he cut a deal with Streck's lawyer for Streck to serve four to eight years, out in three.

Getting rid of the witness had cost Streck a lot of favors. The only reason he copped to the plea was not knowing if someone might change their minds about testifying. Especially since he *had* tried to murder the simple bastard. It was too bad so many people could identify him when he ran the fucker down.

Chapter Four

Bailey was half-pissed off at Travis for the nonchalant attitude he had displayed when Bailey hit him up about the dead horses. Changes would have to be made in the way the herds in the refuge were monitored. And if Bailey moved up to Dennis's job, Travis would be in for a rude awakening.

When Bailey helped set up the wild horse refuge, the idea was for the herds to make it on their own; however, being stranded in a canyon and starving to death wasn't his intention, fuck nature's way.

He had watched the buckskin stallion for three years out there, holding on to his harem, fighting off the younger stallions trying to take his herd.

Even though he wasn't a horseman, Bailey admired the buckskin, and before his life started working towards the sewer, he would watch the herd for hours.

Over the sagebrush and plains the stallion would be in front of the herd, tail high, racing the wind. Bailey envied the freedom and contentment the stallion possessed.

When the drinking started getting out of hand (according to Dana), he spent more and more time out on the refuge, and would begrudgingly start back to town after the sun was well down. When he'd get home, it always seemed like Dana was pissed and the fights would start.

"Bailey," she'd say near tears, "dammit, you can't hide at the refuge forever. We need to work this out. Please, talk to me."

They used to share their problems and work them out until Bailey just quit talking to her about his. Maybe a macho thing, who the hell knew? The fridge door would slam and he'd flop his ass down in the chair in front of the TV. Since then, she'd left.

Bailey picked the phone up and called Roger Horton, head of the local Mental Health and a long-time friend of Bailey's.

"Roger, Bailey. I wonder if I could come over this afternoon and talk to you. Make an appointment for me, this will be professional, not social."

After hanging up, he felt a little better. He knew a marriage of over twenty years didn't go to hell in less than six months on a whim. Getting older and adding a job change with slopping down a six pack of Bud every night had to lead to problems. It had taken Dana leaving to make him realize his problems were deeper than what he wanted to admit.

          *   *   *   *   *   *   *   *   *

Williams arrived and went into his office. After putting his coat and hat on a rack then walking over to the coffeepot, he said good morning to everyone and shook their hands; then he went into the Men's room and washed. He had done the same thing every morning for the two years he had been there.

Williams didn't think it was very sanitary to shake all those hands and not wash afterwards.

Bailey knew his routine and had always been busy when Williams started his ritual, so he'd be passed by. Bailey even knew about the hand washing, having seen him too many times after glad-handing and heading for the head. Bailey would go in and act like he was cleaning his coffee cup and see Williams lathering up. Calhoun wondered why he didn't wear gloves. It would save on water and soap and the warmth he projected would be the same.

26

Bailey put the phone to his ear and waved when Williams worked his way back. Williams waved back and went to the restroom.

Bailey was going to tell Williams he would be gone the next day to check the refuge out. He changed his mind as Williams scowled at him on his way to his office.

No, he thought. *Tonight I'll just tell Dora I'll be gone for the day tomorrow.*

At 3:45 in the afternoon he put his coat on and stopped by Dora's desk. "I'm going to be gone from the office tomorrow, Dora. If John wants to know where I'm at, I'm checking some lease proposals." Holding up a folder of proposals he had taken off Dennis's desk, he waved it back and forth. Work had stopped suddenly when Dennis had his heart attack.

He went into the Mental Health Center on Maple and Seventh Street. It was kind of ironic as this house, before it was converted, was where the last controversial issue had taken place when Bailey was a cop.

*   *   *   *   *   *   *   *   *

Tim Grimes was chasing a car up the main drag of Rawlins. Red lights flashing, siren blaring, they raced around blocks of the residential areas.

"Bailey," Grimes radioed. "Snowfield is running from me. Where you at?"

"I'm coming up Maple Street, Tim. Just passed Third." Bailey's lights and siren were on also. Snowfield lived on the corner of Maple and Seventh.

"He's drunk and beat the piss out of Marcie. We just turned north on Seventh; looks like he's trying to get home."

Bailey slid across the street sideways, stopping in the middle just as Snowfield turned onto Maple. Snowfield slammed on his brakes, nearly hitting Bailey's cop car. Grimes screeched to a stop behind him, blocking Snowfield's car.

Alex Snowfield was a big oil rigger who would get drunk, then come home and brutally beat his wife. Marcie worked as a waitress at the Square Shooters Restaurant downtown and everyone liked her; no one liked Snowfield. They all wondered why she stayed with the bastard.

27

The driver's door flew open and Snowfield jumped out of the car, yelling, "I'm gonna kick some ass, you pigs, so come on!"

Bailey walked up and asked, "How're you doing, Alex?" Then he hit him in the jaw with a straight right. He put his hip into the punch and Snowfield flew backward over the trunk of his car; his head slammed against the back window, knocking him out cold.

Grimes ran up. "Christ, Bailey, you might've killed him!"

"Fuck him, I can hear him breathing."

Grimes ran over to his car and called for an ambulance, and then he called for the night duty sergeant, reporting an injury.

As the ambulance left with a still unconscious Snowfield, Pat Reardon, the night sergeant on duty, told Bailey there might be a hearing on his actions if Snowfield was severely injured or filed charges. Bailey wasn't on Reardon's favorite list, so he just shrugged his shoulders and told him, "Whatever."

The next day Reardon called Bailey in and with a concerned expression on his face, offered Bailey his advice. "Calhoun, it doesn't look like Snowfield is going to press charges; he wants to be left alone when he gets out of the hospital. Listen, Bailey, I've seen you grow meaner and harbor more resentment over the last couple of years than most men do in twenty. It's a job you have to take the good with the bad and leave it here when you go home at night. You don't. I think you should look for another career; this one's eating you alive." Kinder, softer, "You're too old-fashioned, Bailey; you can't do stuff to people like you did to Snowfield, even if they are assholes."

For the first time Bailey felt Reardon was talking to him straight, without any grudges or malevolence.

"I've been thinking the same thing, Pat. It seems that anymore all I do is get more and more pissed—about the system, the courts, and the lying, fucking, lawyers. To tell you the truth, I've been looking around. I should know something in the next month."

Reardon told him he would help with a recommendation. Three weeks later Bailey started for the BLM as a field investigator. A month later, he and

Dana were married.

*   *   *   *   *   *   *   *

Bailey told the receptionist he had an appointment with Roger. She picked up the phone, then sent him down the hallway to what used to be Snowfield's bedroom, but was now Roger's office.

"Come in, Bailey." Roger was holding the door open, a concerned look on his face. "This is quite a surprise; sit down, here." The chair was a big leather recliner, sitting in front of Roger's desk.

"What, no couch?" Bailey thought he made a big mistake coming, but would try it once.

"Only in the movies, my man. What's the problem? You're the last person I ever thought I'd see in here."

"Roger, my life is going to shit in a handbag. Dana's left, I drink at least a six pack of beer every night, and my job sucks."

"Come on, don't butter it up. Tell me flat out what's going on. Sorry, poor time for an attempt at humor. When do you think things started going sour?" Roger leaned back in his chair and opened his hand to Bailey. "I know it's tough to talk about things like this. Just think back to when you started feeling the dissatisfaction."

"I think it started when I lost my ass in the stock market. We had been planning on trying for early retirement until I lost about half of what we had."

"Does Dana keep bringing this up to you? Or is she resentful?"

"Shit no. She just says we'll work a little longer, we wouldn't have been so well off anyway if the market hadn't been acting crazy. And she's right. It's just I felt a little less confined by the job then. I knew in the back of my mind if things got crappy, I could quit and still live pretty good. Course, everything is changed now."

"Did you start drinking more after you lost so much in the market?"

"No, not a lot more. When Williams took the office over, he wanted everything done by the book, which is fine. But after about a year or so, he

29

continually questioned the validity of the refuge. Wondered if it shouldn't revert back to public use. Shit along those kinds of lines. When Dennis announced he was retiring, Williams told me I was going to take his position over, whether I wanted to or not. I got where I'd go to bed and lay there pissed off and not being able to get to sleep. After having a couple of beers, I started sleeping, other than having to get up and piss every couple of hours. Seems like I enjoyed the buzz; I'm mellow, everything's mellow and I sleep. Now I'm knocking down at least a six-pack every night and half the time feel like shit in the morning. This visit probably makes me officially an alcoholic." Bailey slumped down in the chair, almost glaring at Roger in a defensive manner. "I must sound like one hell of a whiner to you, huh? Having a tantrum when I have to go somewhere I don't want to?

"Not at all. If you're good at your job, I can see where you wouldn't want to leave the field for office work. Bailey, I'd be lying if I didn't say you have a serious problem, but recognition and acceptance are the keys. You recognize you're heading for deep shit."

One of the reasons Bailey liked and respected Roger as a psychologist was his straight talking. He sounded real, not an over-educated——impressed with himself——pompous ass.

Bailey left the Center a little after seven in the evening. He had talked more at one time to Roger than he had in the last six months to Dana. He knew what he had to do and wondered if he could. What he thought was how good a beer would taste as he looked over some literature Roger had given him on drinking.

    *   *   *   *   *   *   *   *   *

After Bailey left his office, Roger called Dana at Jenny's house. Bailey had told him she was staying with her friend, whose reputation was one of a strong women's rights advocate and head of a women's abuse shelter.

"Abuse Center, how may I help you?" Jenny answered. She often took shelter calls at home and answered her personal phone in this manner.

"Jenny, this is Roger Horton. May I speak to Dana, please?"

"Hold on a sec, Roger." The phone thumped down on the tabletop.

He knew she was asking Dana if she wanted to talk to him.

After a short pause, "Roger, how are you?" Dana said.

He could feel the suspicion in her voice. "Dana, Bailey was in to see me today. We had quite a talk, a lot about you."

"Oh, does he blame me for what's happening to him?"

"No, no. Quite the opposite. He knows he's got a drinking problem and has been treating you, in his words, 'like rat shit'. What I wanted to tell you was he is going to try to work it out. You need to be supportive but not a crutch. I would like to suggest you stay away for a while even if you and he talk things out. He needs to realize what's at stake. You. If later, you feel he's quit the booze for the right reasons, and if you both would then like to come see me, I think it would be great."

"God, what good news, Roger! I didn't know what else to do except leave. Hopefully, this is the turn in the road. Thank you." If tears could be seen over the phone, Roger would have seen them running silently down Dana's cheeks.

"If there's anything I can do for you, Dana, call me. Please."

"All right, Roger, thanks." She hung the phone up and when Jenny saw her, she flared her famous temper.

"What's up, Dana? Did Roger blame you instead of Bailey? I shouldn't have let him talk to you."

"Good news! Believe it or not, Bailey's talking to Roger. I never thought this could have happened to us, Jenny."

Jenny was nearly five-foot, ten inches tall and towered over Dana's five foot three. "Not to put a damper on what Roger said, but Bailey continuing to be an ass wouldn't surprise me in the least. Don't be too quick to forget, Dana."

Dana was going to the University of Wyoming when she met Bailey. He was taking law enforcement and range management; she was majoring in library science. They dated a few times, and then Bailey joined the Marines after two years of college. She finished her degree and ended up in Rawlins as the Assistant Head Librarian for the County Library. When Bailey got back from overseas and joined the Police Department, they started dating.

They went together until Bailey started work for the BLM and they were married in Las Vegas.

Being from a small town in Iowa, she had a difficult time living in Southern Wyoming, where the wind blew and the plains were wide and sweeping. She didn't quite share Bailey's love of the wild horses, but she understood it, and never complained when it took time away from her, time that could have been spent at home.

A little jealous? Maybe. With the exception of the last six months, the twenty years they had been married left her with satisfaction and contentment. She still loved Bailey, and she knew he loved her; this was just a hurdle the two of them must get over. And, according to Roger, Bailey had to do most of it himself.

Chapter Five

When Bailey woke up the next morning, it was the first time he didn't have a hangover or worse in a long time. He'd slept all night and didn't have to get up every couple of hours and piss.

He made a lunch and put two cans of Bud Light in the cooler (he wasn't sure why), and then had Callie, their half Great Pyrenees, half Heeler, get in the back of the truck.

It was seven in the morning and the sun had been up about an hour. The sky was a brilliant blue and absolutely no clouds could be seen. It was a magnificent April morning.

Heading out north on US 287, the sun to his right, he was always amazed at the great expanse of prairie spread out in front of him. Herds of antelope stood by the side of the highway looking up as he sped by. It was the high plains and when he came to Willow Hill, the highway dropped down a thousand feet in elevation. Four mountain ranges, each a different hue of blue, stood out. The Ferris Mountains to the northeast stood tall like sentries, with granite facings similar to medals on a chest. Green Mountain was to the northwest and encompassed the area he drove toward.

He loosened his grip on the steering wheel when they reached the bottom of Willow Hill and the highway started to straighten out on Separation Flats, a huge bowl of mostly sagebrush and alkali, leaving dirty white smudges stretching out from the rancid pools of water.

As he came through and passed Lamont, he remembered when it had cafes and bars; hell, it even had a school once. Now the school was boarded up, the roof caving in and the only building left besides a couple of trailers was Grandma's Cafe.

About fifteen miles out of Lamont, Bailey turned to the west at Three Forks, then turned south after a couple of miles on a road where a rusted, stained, discarded oil recovery tank stood near the road entrance. Then it was all rough dirt road, driving past a sign with bright white letters stating, "Wild Horse Refuge, no hunting or chasing of wild horses, by order of the Bureau of Land Management."

The refuge was fifty miles north of Rawlins, encompassing the base of Green Mountain to the west and spreading out approximately thirty-five square miles to the east. The only signs of man were the junk oil pumps, barrels and shacks they had abandoned after the oil boom died in the 80's. That's what determined modern man, how much crap he left behind him.

Bailey pulled the lever into four-wheel drive to get through some of the washes and banks where they had caved in on the road. Controlling the spin on the tires, he finally made his way through the arroyos, canyons and plains that made up the terrain of the refuge. He located the dirt road he needed to take to get up to the top of a small box canyon and crept up to the crest. Tires slipped and spit rocks out when he finally stopped short of the ridge.

It would have been easier and faster to walk up here, he thought. Getting out of the truck and letting the dog jump out, he walked to the edge of the rim.

"Jesus Christ." Down below him were the bodies of horses lying in the grass and rocks. He counted fifteen dead wild horses. Of the fifteen, nine were yearling colts.

He started climbing down the outcroppings, taking his time, as the footing was treacherous. When he finally reached the bottom, the smell of death and decay was horrendous. Gagging and nearly throwing up, he walked

34

among the dead mustangs. His head pounded with blood like a migraine headache coming on. Bailey felt his chest tighten and his breathing became labored.

"You low life pieces of shit! What kind of fucking cowards would do this?" His voice was a low rasp, the emotion nearly choking him. The dog bolted from the fierce tone. He took a deep breath.

"You better hope to God I never find you," he said in a murderous tone. He felt such a rage, such a desire to get the horse killers; the realization he had never been so pissed off before in his life made him clinch his jaw until it hurt. It seemed as if all his frustrations were being channeled into one focal point. It almost felt good.

He pulled his pocketknife out and dug bullets from the bodies. Judging by the marks in the ground made from thrashing and the angles of the horses, he knew they had died painfully. There were few clean-looking kills. He noticed many of the horses had what looked like tearstains on their faces. *Jesus, can horses cry?* It damned near suffocated him with all the emotion he felt. Bailey knew in his soul someone would pay. And pay dearly. When he had bullets from all fifteen horses he looked over and saw his dog's legs in the air.

"Callie, what the hell are you doing?" He ran over to her. She was rolling on the bodies of two colts, her fur showing a slight dirty streak on the back and sides. "For Christ's sake, get back to the truck, dammit." He swatted her on the butt as she ran for the side of the canyon.

When he climbed back up to the top, he walked the rim and found a half-dozen .223 casings scattered about. He picked them up and added them to the bullets in a large baggy he brought. He looked around for some kind of sign, but the wind and snow had obliterated any possibility of tracks being left. He went to the truck and taking his binoculars out, looked to the south, where another faint road went.

He saw a glint of red by some sand dunes. "Old Frank is at it again," he mumbled to himself. He drove up to the dunes where an old, red beat-up jeep was sitting. The top was made from wood and there was one tire that was a size too small on the front.

"Frank, where the hell are you?"

"You scared hell out of me, Bailey." This came from the rumpled figure of an old man creeping out from under a tall chunk of sagebrush.

"I was afraid it was Knight, and he don't treat me like you do." He put a cloth bag down and squinted as he looked at Bailey.

"I haven't seen ya in a couple of months. Figured you quit or someone ran your ass off. Where the hell you been?" Frank asked.

"Climbing the stairs of government advancement. What you got in the sack, Frank?"

"Just some skinning stones, couple of warheads and a nice spearhead, not a nick on it," the old man replied.

"Dammit, Frank, you know you aren't supposed to take stuff; it's protected, they're antiquities." Bailey was exasperated. He had let Frank pilfer the artifacts in the past because he kept Bailey in the groove on some of the things going on out there. Like having an extra set of eyes. Frank would sell the artifacts and it would help him with supplies, but he wasn't supposed to do it to excess. If Frank was around the sand dunes, then he was looking because the dunes were where the Indians had camped nearly 150 years ago. He had an old shack on Green Mountain where he lived year-around and Bailey always thought he would find him dead there, an old man who didn't change with the times and seemed to enjoy it.

"Frank, I found fifteen horses over below Riley's Ridge. They've been shot, you know anything about it?"

"If I told you something, I oughta be able to take what I want from around here without any of your shit, Bailey."

"You tell first, then I'll decide how much stuff you get."

"Last week or so I was down here and heard some shooting going on from that direction." He pointed to the north with a dirt-encrusted finger, "Saw a truck coming a little bit later, this way. I hid my jeep around the dune; they went right by me, taking their time."

"Did you know them?" Bailey could feel the stir of excitement building up in his body. He went over to his truck and got a beer out and gave it to Frank.

36

"Bud Light, normally don't have this premium beer, costs too much."

He popped the top and took a big pull, smacked his lips and ran his tongue down along his beard to pick up what drops might have spilled.

"It was a white and brown Ford, I think, I don't know the brands much, but I seen it out here before." He took another swallow and let loose with a loud raucous belch. "Aaah, that's good beer, you got anymore?"

Bailey reached into the cooler and pulled another can out, holding it in his hand as he asked, "Come on Frank, what else you see?"

Eyeing the beer he looked around like they were in a crowd of people and he didn't want anyone to hear. "There was three guys in it, but I didn't know none of 'em. Looked like one of them trucks you used to see out here; you know, the ones the oil outfits used to haul the crews to the rigs, but it weren't new, it was pretty beat up."

"Okay, now you earned half the stuff in the bag, now what do you have to get you the other half?" Bailey thought he heard a vehicle off in the distance, but the sound died just as suddenly as it had started.

"There was a hell of lot of shootin' about four, five days ago, west of the old stage stop, but I never went over around there and I didn't see nothing."

Bailey just stared at him, not saying a word, waiting.

"All right, goddammit! There's a bunch of dead horses over in the small box canyon, one where the sheepherder's marker's on the top."

Years ago the sheepherders used to mark where their sheep were grazing by putting stacks of stones holding a chunk of wood sticking out on the top of a hill. Since they were usually on horseback, it gave them a way to keep their bearings by looking up and seeing the markers from quite a distance away.

"If there's a reward for any of this stuff, I expect to get it, Calhoun."

"Frank, get your stuff and get out of here; you're pissing me off right now." His lips were tight, jaws clenched.

"Sure, Calhoun, I was leaving anyway." He threw the beer can to the ground.

"Pick it up, Frank, that's not our state flower. Stick it in your pocket and go."

Frank stepped on the can, flattening it, then picked it up and stuck it in his back pocket. "See ya, Calhoun," he said over his shoulder as he hobbled back to his jeep. He got in with a grunt, fired the engine, then in a wake of blue, oily smoke, he slowly drove down the road towards the direction of his shack.

Bailey watched him leave and then contemplated his next move. It was getting late; in early April the sun started going down around 6:00 p.m. and once it dropped behind the hills the shadows lengthened and it started getting cold, particularly if the wind was blowing. The wind had picked up in the afternoon so he decided to go back to town that evening. In the morning he would check with Carl Toomes about flying him over the area the coming weekend.

Carl used to fly for the Cattlemen's Association, killing coyotes. They quit using him when the government quit paying the bounty. He'd usually take Bailey up if he paid for the fuel. If there was an eight by hundred-foot half-flat strip of land, Carl would drop his Super Cub down like a World War Two flying ace strafing a bridge. He would scare the crap out of Bailey once in a while, but there wasn't anyone else he would trust to fly and land out there.

Bailey put Callie in the back of the pickup, then drove south down the old washed-out road towards Lamont. He'd come in from the west directly across from the café. He thought he'd stop and eat there. One good thing was if there weren't any customers, or ones who weren't from around the area, then Minnie McGuire, the owner, chief cook and bottle washer, would let Callie come in and lay by the door, usually with a big meaty bone to gnaw on.

Minnie was a short, squatty, one-quarter Mexican, three-quarter Irish woman who would give you the shirt off her back. She was probably fifty or so, but still had coal black hair, though it was probably coal black from the bottle. She'd had the café for ten years and Bailey would always eat there when he was out on the job.

Callie perked up and started whining when they drove into the parking

38

area in front of the restaurant. There was only one car in the parking lot, and by the looks of the car, they wouldn't mind if Bailey and Callie joined in for dinner. The aroma of pot roast filtered through the door when they walked in. Bailey's mouth salivated from the memory of how good the pot roast always was.

"Minnie, how about two plates of roast? One for me and one for my friend."

"Sure, Bailey, I've got a bone for you and a plate for Callie." She giggled at her own humor as she unwedged herself from behind the cash register stand, where she had been reading one of the rag sheets.

"Any alien babies being born, as reported in the National Peek?" Bailey tried making his voice sound like Walter Winchell.

"Not yet, but I wouldn't be surprised if they found proof one of these days," Minnie sniffed. She took her papers seriously.

She poured him a cup of coffee without asking and then set a bone down for Callie by the door. "Whew, what's she been in? Good thing there's no customers." She waddled back behind the counter and scooped up a huge ladle of pot roast (it was more like stew) and dumped it into a large bowl; expertly put together a salad, took some french bread out of the oven and set it all down in front of him.

"Bailey, I'll sit by you and give you some dinner company if you don't try to get fresh." She giggled again as she sat down by him.

"Minnie, have you seen three guys around here lately, driving an old white and brown Ford truck? Maybe stopped for some food or beer?"

"Well now, come to think of it, there was some fellas like you're talking about come in last week. They weren't very nice, had some pretty foul language. This one guy, he wants an Old Sheridan beer. No decent place would stock it. I told him we carry Bud, Bud Light, Coors and Millers and nothing else. They bought a six-pack of Bud and left. I was glad to see them go, because I was here alone." Her eyes twinkled and she got a little grin, "Of course, I had my old shotgun right beside me, under the counter."

"What did they look like?" He pulled a notebook out of his shirt pocket and picked up a pen off the counter.

"Well, one was big, about your height, but heavier, had a tattoo on his neck. Never seen a tattoo on somebody's neck before, have you? Anyhow, the other two were just a couple of dirty looking guys, 'cept they were bundled up to their chins and had their hats pulled down low. I thought at first they were going to rob me. The big guy was the honcho; he told them what to do, and I never heard them say anything. They might not even of spoke English."

Bailey wrote it down, then not able to get any more out of her, he finished his dinner. After paying the check, he left a large tip.

"Bailey, you sly devil, you're trying to buy my love, you sweetheart", Minnie said.

He smiled at her. "Minnie, these guys come back or if you see them around anywhere, call me, will you? Anytime."

"What's going on, Bailey? Is it trouble?"

"I'll be in next week for dinner and we'll have a talk about it, but until then don't say anything to anyone about my asking about these guys. By the way, whose old car is out front? There's no one in here."

"I don't know; it was just here one morning, no license plates, just sitting there making my place look bad. I'm going to have the Patrol move it or something. See if they can tow it off my property. Unless it's a cute little Mexican fella looking for a larger, more mature woman to care of him." Her face brightened up, maybe even blushed a bit.

She has to be lonely out here, especially in the winter, Bailey thought as he walked to his truck. Callie still stunk to high heaven, so he put her in the truck bed, and took off for Rawlins.

With every vehicle he saw going the opposite way, he would squint into the headlights and try to see if it was a white and brown Ford pickup, with three people in it. But he never saw one; the lights always blinded him first.

He pulled into Rawlins about 8:30 p.m.; the wind had picked up and the temperature had dropped, clouds started rolling in and he thought there was a good chance for a spring snow. He might have to postpone his plane ride. Hopefully not, Bailey thought, weekends might be his only chance to go. He knew he was going to have to watch his ass after the confrontations with Williams, so there wouldn't be any flying during working hours.

He came in on the highway and turned north on Palmer Place. The street was three blocks long, lined with aspen and western fir trees and ended in a cul-de-sac. His and Dana's house was the first one on the second block facing south. It was a one-level ranch with a single garage, now containing Bailey's shop, and the basement was partially finished. Just his office, a couple of chairs, a TV and a bathroom with a small shower.

He pulled into the driveway and shut his truck off. The dog jumped against the gate as he opened it.

"Night, Callie, hope you had a good time, clean the stink off yourself, okay?" He made sure she had food and water, then went into his house through the kitchen. He took his jacket off and pitched it on the kitchen chair——this always pissed Dana off——and got a beer and some chicken out of the fridge. The beer can felt comfortable in his hand and would feel better going down his throat. Surprising himself, he put it back in the refrigerator then remembered he left the bag with the bullets in his truck. The bag was fairly heavy and made a sound like marbles rolling down a sheet of metal when he laid them out on the kitchen table. Some were encrusted with blood and pieces of hair. He had recovered twenty-seven bullets. They were in good enough shape to get some ballistics for comparisons with other bullets.

Why would some guys go out and do this? It doesn't feel like someone is doing it for the thrill. He wrote a note to himself to contact the Sheriff's Office in Rock Springs the next day and talk to the deputy who investigated the shootings over there last week. He gathered the bullets and casings and carefully wrapped them in a towel then put them in a baggy and placed it over by the wood next to the fireplace.

He drank some coke and thought about calling Dana, but remembered she didn't want him calling her until he had things worked out. *I'm not gonna push my luck yet.*

The coke in his hand brought a thoughtful sigh. *This doesn't compare to a Bud.* He finished the drink and decided to go to bed early. The feeling of long days to come working on the case gave him a tinge of excitement. The

41

same kick an old racehorse had before the starting bell rang. If he was going to contend with Williams, Dana, and a bunch of dead wild horses, he better have his shit together.

Chapter Six

Lynch and Gomez were in the pen for burglarizing a Circuit City store in Lakewood that specialized in computers and cameras. They might have walked away except Lynch got a video camera from one of the shelves and videotaped Gomez picking up a camera box and putting two digital cameras down his shirt. Then he turned it on himself, and said, "Hearrrrrrs Jackson!"

They were just getting into their car to leave when the cops showed up, and the rest was history.

They weren't known as the brightest of criminals. They also didn't have a conscience when it came to hurting someone, especially if the money was good. And to them, if they got $2500 each, they would kill whomever the payer wanted. They didn't have any violent crimes on their rap sheet, but they had made some money the old-fashioned way, they'd killed for it.

Streck had met them in the mess hall of the pen. He sat down by them one day and slowly ate his food. Between bites he said, "Didn't you guys do some work for Ruben Madrid?"

They looked at each other, then Gomez said, "You know Ruben? We call him split face cuz of the knife scar he got along his cheek."

43

"Nice try, dipshit, Madrid don't have no scar on his face."

"Why do you want to know?" said Lynch, looking straight down into his food tray, not lifting his head up, not wanting to give Streck the idea he might be challenging him.

"I'm getting out next month and starting up a little business, consultant type. Everyone I know who worked for Madrid kept their mouths shut. I'm looking for someone like that; already got some leads on some work."

"Whatta you mean, consultant work?"

Streck looked them over, then lowered his voice a bit,

"I'm gonna help people fix problems, in fact, no problem too big or small. Get my drift?" Streck looked at them, no humor in his eyes. "I've got some connections in Denver, they're gonna refer me."

"We're getting out the same time as you." Lynch still kept his eyes down and just kept shoveling the food into his mouth.

"When you leave, give us a number," he said between bites.

After that day, Streck sat with them at their table every meal; he still didn't say a whole hell of a lot, but Lynch and Gomez also noticed they didn't get any more shit from the other inmates. Maybe this little business arrangement had some potential.

The day before Streck was to be released, he ate the evening meal with Lynch and Gomez. Handing Lynch a piece of paper, he stared at both of them hard.

"You can get ahold of me by calling this number. It ain't for anybody else. You give it anybody else and you're dead, understand me?"

"You don't need to talk to us that way; we ain't gonna tell a soul. Right, Gomez? Couple of weeks from now we'll be drinking beer down at Sonny's and hooking up with some puss." Lynch showed his teeth in a big grin, one front tooth missing and the rest dark yellow and stained; they looked like he had been eating rocks, with chips and ragged tops.

"When I get some money ahead, I'm gonna get my teeth done, like Gomez's. Nice and white and straight." Lynch said.

Lynch knew Gomez was proud of his teeth, always giving a big smile if Lynch was around.

Gomez flashed a big smile, taking in Streck and Lynch.

"You bet, this is gonna work out good for all of us." Gomez said.

Lynch picked up his tray, sticking the note in his pocket with a deft, practiced movement to keep the guards from seeing and started walking away. "Later."

*   *   *   *   *   *   *   *   *

"Okay, Streck. Time to leave our happy family." The guard said on Wednesday morning.

The gate opened and he walked out with his bag of personal possessions and a hundred dollars in his pocket, courtesy of the fine State of Colorado. The girl he had used for years, sometimes hooker, Patsy Mae Brinkman, met him.

"Streck, over here!" A hand waved frantically in the parking lot.

Patsy Mae had been with Streck off and on for the last six years and had stayed in contact with him the last three while he was in prison. He told her not to visit, but he allowed her to send him money when he needed it.

"God, I've missed you. How do I look?" She was tall, thin and not pretty. Patsy Mae had washed-out, dull, blond hair and acne scars thick on her cheeks.

"Just fine, Patsy Mae. Now let's quit the bullshit and get me the hell out of here."

He had a hold over her like so many men do over women who are ill-equipped to make it in the outside world without the berating, belittling, mental abuse so often unnoticed and uncared about in their part of society.

He got into her car, a 1978 Buick LeSabre 4-door, the color of muddy water, with the right front fender caved in below the headlight, rust streaks down the trunk and a dirty white roof. She got in the driver's side, started the car, looked over at him and said, "You been in the joint for three years, Streck, ya want to go to a motel first?"

"Patsy Mae, let's get to Denver first, then we'll look at having some

45

action. I need to get away from here...now."

She put the car into drive, made a U-turn and drove down Highway 50 until she came to I-25, then she took the northbound exit and accelerated onto the interstate. With a little shimmy in the steering wheel, she soon had the Buick up to 75 mph. With one hand on the wheel, she reached under her seat with her right hand and pulled out a small vial.

"Take a snort, Streck, maybe it'll loosen you up some."

He took the vial in his hand and twisted the top off. He pressed the window down button, then threw the coke out.

She looked at him with disbelief.

"What the hell are you doing? You crazy? You just threw out a hundred bucks worth of some pretty good shit."

Streck eased his hand to the back of her neck and started stroking it slowly up and down, then to the side a little harder.

"If you weren't driving this car right now, I'd beat the shit out of you so bad you wouldn't wake up for a week. Do you think I'm going to take a chance on getting caught with dope twenty minutes after I get out of the joint? You're stupider than I ever gave you credit for. Now I don't want to hear a word out of your ignorant mouth until we get to Denver. Got it? Don't say anything, just nod your fuckin head yes!" He sounded furious and he was almost screaming the last to her.

She nodded her head up and down. "I'm sorry Streck, I screwed up. I didn't think. I — I can see why you'd be pissed at me, but don't hurt me, okay?"

The next two and a half-hours were ridden in silence with just the noise of a bearing getting worse in the transmission.

When they got to Denver they pulled up to a dumpy old apartment house on Logan Street. There was trash in the yard and it looked as if what grass was there had never been mowed. Streck grabbed his bag and followed Patsy Mae into the entryway, and then they walked up two flights and went down the corridor to 3C.

She unlocked the apartment door and started in, keeping her back to him and not saying anything.

Her head snapped forward and she saw stars. A hand grabbed her around the neck and flung her onto the floor in front of a threadbare couch.

"Don't, Streck! I'm sorry, Christ, I'm sorry!" She whimpered.

He looked down on her. "If I didn't have things to do I'd rip your ass good. Here's twenty-five bucks, get yourself cleaned up, then go get some groceries. I'll be back to eat around seven." He opened the door and walked through.

"You better get your shit together, Patsy Mae."

She could hear him stomping down the stairs. She picked herself up and went into the bathroom; running some water, she rinsed a washcloth and put it to the back of her head.

"Asshole, you'll get yours someday." Then the tears started as they always did when someone beat her up, and she left to buy some food.

Streck walked down East Colfax to the Capital Hill area and slipped into the Idle Hours Bar. He sided up to the bar and waited for the bartender to get his order. It was a little after three.

"Hey Streck, how's it going? Just get out?" The bartender put a shot of Old Crow down with a beer chaser.

"Yeah, just got back. Looking for Tommy, seen him around?"

The bartender, who was an ex-con himself, nodded his head. He didn't say anything, but pointed to a door at the back of the bar, just past the kitchen entry. Streck downed his Crow then took a big swallow of beer as he got up and swaggered to the back. Lightly rapping on the door, he opened it when he heard "Enter.."

Tommy "Blade" Pastroli was sitting behind a large oak desk that held an office phone and nothing else. Bare as a baby's butt. He had broad shoulders, no neck and receding, grayish black hair. His face was wide with a nose showing it had been broken several times. He could stop someone in their tracks with his piercing blue eyes when he stared at them.

Tommy was an enforcer for the mob in Denver and had risen to the moderate rank where he delegated the enforcing. The nickname "Blade" came from using a knife to make his point on deadbeats who didn't pay their debts and to permanently take care of those who his bosses wanted out of this world, for whatever reason. No one screwed with him and he used different people not in the mob to do some freelance work. That's what he used Streck for — freelance; and if he got caught, he wouldn't squeal; he knew the rules. It also wouldn't be a big loss since Streck was a fucking psycho.

"Streck, good to see ya. Ya said you were ready for some work, right?" He turned his back to him and pulled a sheet of paper out of his briefcase. "Need you to give this guy a little lesson; he likes to bet, but he doesn't like to pay off when he loses. This is where he works." He pointed to an address on the paper. "I'm working on a deal out of state; if things work out, I'll give you a call — it'll be big bucks."

"What kind of lesson, not walk for a while or a couple of broken fingers?"

"Just do the fingers; this guy owns a carpet wholesale place and if we make it where he don't walk, then he can't make much money. He just thought he was a little smarter in betting than he was. I want him to know he has to pay by the end of the week, or there'll be more than his fingers broke." He gave the paper to Streck. "This is worth $500, here's half, you get the rest when it's done."

"I wouldn't expect any less." Running his finger down the sheet of paper, he asked, "What's he look like?"

"He's a big guy, about six foot or so, 200-220 lbs., he's a little paunchy, has slicked-back, blond hair and he drives a new Volvo wagon. Brown and gold. That what's really pisses me off; I mean, he can drive a new car, but can't pay me my money. He goes by 'Bobby.' He might have a wife with him but don't hurt her; she's a little blond about twenty years younger than him. Let him know she'll be the next one if he doesn't pay."

"Okay, I'll go over tonight, pay him a visit. This's right off 58th and I-25, ain't it?"

Pastroli nodded his head.

"You got any wheels I can use? I had to get rid of mine to pay my lawyer."

Pastroli rummaged through his top desk drawer and threw a set of keys onto the top of his desk.

"Blue '86 Pontiac Bonneville, it's clean so far; the plates on it are from a wrecking yard. Use it while you're here."

Picking up the keys and turning to leave, he told Pastroli thanks and left the room. Going through the bar he nodded at the bartender who waved back with his palm close to the bar, moving it sideways. An old con sign of *everything's cool*. He walked through the alley and found the car. Getting in, he started it and drove out of the alley turning on Morey Avenue. The afternoon traffic increased as he converged with a thousand other cars and turned west on Colfax then turned north on Speer Blvd., staying on it until he got onto I-25 north where he stayed in the right hand lane until he took the 58th Street exit. He saw the Denver Merchandise Mart and pulled into the parking lot. He gave it the once-over and saw what looked like a private parking area. Scouring it, he glimpsed a brown and gold Volvo wagon, the license numbers matching what he had down on the paper. He backed up against the curb in the corner adjacent to where the Volvo was parked and waited.

About six, Bobby came walking out, swinging his briefcase and carrying a leather overcoat, heading towards the Volvo.

Streck got out and started walking towards Bobby, who had the back of the wagon open and was jamming his briefcase between a set of golf clubs.

"Excuse me," Streck muttered as he walked up.

Bobby rose up to see who was talking, when he was hit in the stomach with Streck's fist. Bobby's wind blew out as he dropped to the ground, doubled over. Streck kicked him in the ribs, knocking him into the side of the car. "You got a debt to pay, do it by Friday or I'll visit your old lady." He reached down, grabbed Bobby's middle two fingers of his left hand and with quick, backward thrust snapped both them just below his knuckles. Bobby let out a high scream and cradled his fingers now sticking back at an awkward angle. Streck stepped to the side and kicked out a taillight on the car, then walked over to the Pontiac and left in a screech of rubber.

49

He went up to Federal and turned south, merging with the traffic. Stopping at a drive-thru liquor store, he bought a fifth of Old Crow and a six pack of Old Sheridan beer, then drove back to the apartment at a leisurely pace. He'd wait a few days then go back to Tommy's and collect the last $250; not bad pay for a little over two hours' work, including the drive.

When he got to the apartment, it was surprisingly empty. He figured Patsy Mae was either getting food or trying to pick up a late trick. He poured a water glass half full of the whiskey and opened a can of beer, then sat down at the wooden kitchen table and sipped his drink. The kitchen window looked over Logan Street and he saw a couple of guys walking up the street, nattily dressed.

Looks like a couple of pimps, probably looking for Patsy Mae, he thought. I gotta have her pick up Lynch and Gomez Tuesday.

He saw a telephone by the couch and was surprised it worked. He dialed a number he knew by heart and when a voice answered by repeating the number, he spoke in a soft, low tone. "This is Streck, I need you to pass on to Lynch and Gomez in B Block they got a ride waiting when they get out Tuesday."

"That'll cost you a hundred bucks, how you going to pay?"

"This is for the Blade, you bill him for it if you got the balls."

There was a click and the phone went dead. He hung up and knew the message would get passed. There was an advantage to working for a well-known, mean bastard.

Patsy Mae opened the door as he was hanging the phone up.

"Hey, Streck, don't make no long distance calls, okay? I'm hardly paying the phone bill now." She had a small Safeway's grocery sack she put on the counter. Unloading the sack she pulled some hamburger out and two boxes of hamburger helper. Her face brightened up. "You want macaroni and cheese helper or casserole?"

"I want steak!" Streck's face turned red and he started yelling. "Jesus Christ, Patsy Mae, I ate shit like that for three years. Now get your ass out of here and bring me back a big steak, bring some taters too." His voice changed to a lower threatening tone.

"You better not have spent all the bucks I gave you on dope or you're gonna be in deep fuckin' shit."

Patsy Mae moved fast when she thought she might get hit so she was out the door before he could stand up.

She's getting more ignorant every fucking minute. I think we're going to be parting company soon. He got up from the kitchen chair and walked back to the bedroom. Clothes strewn about, dirty clothes on the bed and makeup bottles taking up most of the top of the single, chipped chest of drawers. *Jesus, what a pigsty.* He threw the clothes off the bed onto the floor and laid down. As he drifted off to sleep he thought about how he was going to ditch Pasty Mae and do it where she wouldn't squeal on him. As tough as Streck was, he knew there wasn't anything as bad as a woman sorely pissed off at a man, especially one who'd been fucked over.

He woke up hearing dishes rattling in the kitchen. At first he thought he was back in prison then realization set in. Grunting with the effort of getting out of the broken-down mattress, Streck got up and walked into the kitchen where Patsy Mae was frying a thick steak. The light was a little dim from the 60-watt light bulb hanging down from the center of the kitchen ceiling, but it helped to hide the despair the room emitted. Patsy Mae put the steak on a plate with a stack of french fries and placed it in front of him.

"This ought to be just the way you like it." She had a high lilt to her voice, her eyes looking hollow but bright.

She's stoned, probably used my money. "Got any change?"

"No, the steak and stuff's damn expensive when you go down to Seymours' on the corner. I think he's a Jew."

Streck ate in silence but his eyes followed her as she flitted around the room. *I think, Patsy Mae, after you pick up the boys, we're definitely parting company.* "I'm gonna give you a hundred bucks and have you go down to Canyon City again and pick a couple of guys up for me Tuesday, okay? This'll take care of gas and you can get a couple of things for yourself." Streck pulled a roll of bills out and gave her several.

Pasty Mae looked at him in disbelief.

Streck knew with the extra money, she'd score some dope for herself.

Can Horses Cry?

The stupid bitch probably thinks I'm finally coming around. Yeah, she thinks I'm gonna tie up with her permanently, he thought.

Friday morning Streck woke up about seven and eased himself out of bed. Getting dressed he left the apartment as quiet as a thief; he didn't want to have to screw with Patsy Mae right then because he had some business to take care of. He pulled away in the Pontiac and drove south to Colfax, then turned west and maneuvered in the rush hour traffic until he worked his way onto Speer Blvd., then I-25 north. He stayed in the right-hand lane, took the 58th Street exit and went back to the parking lot of the Merchandise Mart. He parked away from the entrance and settled back to see if Bobby was going to show up. He wanted to know if he had the fear in him. The fear of Streck. Around eight, the Volvo drove in and parked in the restricted lot. Bobby got out, his left hand sporting a cast from his wrist to his two middle fingers. His face looked haggard as he pulled his briefcase out of the back seat and started walking towards the entrance to the building.

Streck got out of his car and hollered, "You pay yet, dipshit?"

Bobby jumped sideways, holding his briefcase up protectively to his chest and his face drained of color.

"Yes, I swear. I paid yesterday!" Fear resonated from him.

"That's all I want to know; get your ass out of here."

Bobby raced to the front door then slowed to a walk as he opened the door and went in. Streck chuckled to himself; *the chicken-shit doesn't have any balls.* He sauntered back to his car and decided to drive down to DIA. He'd never been out there and it would kill some time until he could go see Tommy. He wanted the two hundred fifty bucks and hopefully the other job would be waiting.

The shadows were lengthening and sun was drifting down behind the mountains when Streck walked into the bar. He nodded to the same bartender in the direction of Tommy's office and received a quick shake of the head. He walked back and knocked on the door.

"Enter."

As he walked in Tommy pulled a wad of bills out from his coat pocket and peeled off two hundred-dollar bills and a fifty.

52

"Good work, the little wimp came in the next morning with his cast on and paid me." Pastroli chuckled. "I got a job for you if you want it. Up in Wyoming. Shouldn't take you more than three, four weeks and you'll get $40,000. You gotta pay your own expenses, though, and you're gonna need some bodies who know the ropes. You'll have to pay them yourself."

Streck sat down and took a sip of the whiskey Tommy had poured him. "This a connected job?" He had implied the mob being involved and was surprised when Tommy said yes.

An hour later he left the bar and got into the Bonneville he had negotiated for in the deal. With the exception of no title and stolen plates, it was his. He fought the traffic but only to Logan Street where he turned into the slow traffic lane and drove to the apartment.

Tuesday night around seven, Patsy Mae, Lynch and Gomez showed up at the apartment. The three were stoned and it was all Streck could do to keep from murdering all of them.

Sitting down at the kitchen table, Streck explained what was going on. "I've got us a job up in Wyoming for about three weeks. It pays $2,000 a week and expenses. If you're in, we leave tomorrow."

"So what do you wanna do?" Lynch asked Gomez.

Lynch sucked a long drag down his throat from the joint, held it in his lungs for a bit, then exhaled it out very slowly.

"Don't worry, Streck, I ain't inhaling." He started chuckling at his own joke, and then smiled at Streck.

"We're in, right Gomez?"

Gomez, nodding his head, said, "When are we leaving?"

"In the morning. Patsy Mae and me are going out on the town tonight and you guys can go find some pussy or whatever."

Patsy Mae quickly looked up at Streck, a smile forming on her lips,

"Give me ten minutes to get pretty for you." She went into the bathroom.

Streck knew ten years wouldn't be enough time to make herself pretty.

53

Her eyes had dark blue eye shadow on her upper lids and she put something in her hair to make it give off a soft, golden glitter. Her outfit was clean and didn't look like the normal hooker clothes she wore all of the time.

"I'm ready, Streck. So long, you guys, I'm gonna have me a great night!" She put her arm through Streck's and gave a toss of her head. "I seen the movie stars do that on TV," she said, her arm through Streck's as they left the apartment.

"Well, Juan, whatda you say we go out and get us some puss?" Gomez showed his agreement by putting on his coat and holding the door for Lynch. Lynch put his arm through Gomez's and threw his head back. They were laughing as they descended the stairs.

       *   *   *   *   *   *   *   *   *

The sound of metal slamming into a solid object woke Gomez and Lynch. They were blurry-eyed and hung over, not knowing if they scored a woman or not. They really didn't give a crap either. Lynch lifted himself off the couch and peered out the window; he noticed Streck at the kitchen table, drinking coffee.

"What the hell's going on out there?" he grumbled. "Ahh, shit, just a fender bender. Come on, Gomez, get your ass up."

Gomez lifted his head from the floor and staggered to the bathroom, not saying a word. A moment later the sound of a large quantity of liquid was heard flowing into the toilet.

"We're leaving in an hour," Streck said as he finished his coffee. "Patsy Mae had to leave early for work, said to say so long."

Lynch nodded his head and went to the bathroom behind Gomez. An hour later Lynch and Gomez were driving Patsy Mae's Buick and Streck was driving the Pontiac, heading north.

Chapter Seven

Bailey got up the next morning with a plan in mind. He was going to call the Sheriff's Office in Rock Springs and try to talk to the deputy investigating the horse shootings over there last week. Then he was going to bounce Travis about the *winterkilled* horses.

Bailey dressed and drove down to the Rustler's for breakfast then came back to the house. After looking in his notebook, he dialed the Rock Springs Sheriff's Office.

Two rings. "Sheriff's Office, Deputy Clark speaking, how can I help you?"

"Deputy Clark, this is Bailey Calhoun, I'm an investigator with the BLM in Rawlins. I'd like to talk to the investigating deputy who's handling the wild horse killings."

"I'm sorry, sir, you want Deputy Maes and he's off for the day. He should be in tomorrow."

"Okay, I'll try in the morning and if I miss him or he's gone, I'll call Monday." Thanking the deputy, Bailey thought he'd go into work and hit

Travis up.

He was the only one there when he went in. Not having looked at them, he put the lease proposals back on Dennis's desk where he had taken them two days before. Fifteen minutes later, Williams came in and went into his office. There were just the two of them when he knocked on Williams's door.

"John, I'd like to talk to you about those dead horses Travis found out at the refuge." Bailey stood by the doorjamb.

"Bailey, we've discussed how I want things to transcend from here." Williams stood up; tall, thin-faced with gold rimmed glasses he always adjusted, and clothes pressed and creased sharp. His hair was thinning and combed straight back, giving him a severe look.

"The refuge shouldn't be your area of interest anymore. I want to give Travis the responsibility and experience out in the field, without undue criticism. Eventually he's going to replace you, and you will be the assistant regional supervisor, my right-hand man, just like Dennis is — was," he said with a tight smile. Williams always seemed to struggle with himself to be civil to Bailey, particularly when he discussed the upcoming promotion.

Dennis had a grandfather's face with silver hair, combed just so. His voice was soft; in fact, so soft a person had to lean in a bit to hear everything he said. Just opposite from Bailey. Everything about Bailey was opposite from Dennis. The difference between the two was what seemed to bother Williams so much.

If Williams's future plans for him were accurate, Bailey had about two months left before his imprisonment as a member of the higher echelon. It would be the same as solitary confinement.

"I don't want you making Travis feel like you're watching every thing he does. So...no, I don't think we have anything to discuss about Travis at the present time."

"Come on, John. You're talking bullshit. He said he found some horses winterkilled and they were shot. I don't think Travis even checked them, and fuck him if he thinks I'm checking up on him."

"Calhoun, I'm tired of your foul mouth and arguing with every decision

56

I make. I'm sure there's a reasonable explanation and being the Regional Supervisor, I'll ask him about it. I've told you what I expect and what I want from you. If you don't want to do it or don't like it, then maybe you should look at early retirement or another career, though at your age it might be hard to accomplish." Williams acted like a judge who had just handed down a sentence to his worst enemy. Satisfied.

Some people might have thought Bailey wasn't very bright, but he wasn't stupid. He held his hands up.

"Hey, hey. I'm sorry. I have some personal things going on I'm not handling very well." Bailey allowed his eyes to drop to the floor. "I'll try to clean up my act." He looked up at Williams.

Williams put his hand on Bailey's back, "I'm glad to hear you say that, Bailey. There's some issues you and I need to resolve and I think maybe this is the first step, thanks." Williams's chest appeared to have puffed out a bit.

The little pretentious prick.

With his face red from anger and embarrassment, Bailey spent the morning going over future budget requests. He noticed Travis hadn't come in yet and he picked up the phone and called across the office to Williams's secretary.

"Dora, where's Travis today? I needed to show him some things." He had a pen and was writing furiously on a piece of paper in case Dora wondered why he would call her rather than walk over.

"Mr. Williams gave him some comp days. I believe he'll be back in the office Monday or Tuesday."

Shortly before noon he thought he'd go to lunch and hopefully avoid Williams the rest of the day. At least he'd have the weekend to calm down.

Bailey went to the Rustler's Restaurant on the east side of town where the food wasn't too bad and the service better than most places. A lot of the office people from the Golden Eagle ate there. He went in and asked for a booth.

"Smoking or non-smoking?" the hostess asked.

"Non," he said, *For Christ's sake, I come in here about four days a week and she asks me every day*. He squinted at her; *she must be Travis's sister*.

He sat down and looked around to see who was there. Low and behold, the Golden Dick himself was just leaving the smoking section. Calvin Knight, resident and owner of the Golden Eagle Oil and Exploration Company, and one of the prominent people of Rawlins.

He had come to town with an oilrig back in the early '60s and had the guts to buy some leases for oil exploration. He hocked everything he had to rent a rig; he struck gas, parlayed it into some oil discoveries and now had a company that drilled, pumped, distilled and ran its products through a pipeline to Denver. No one knew how much Calvin was worth—probably a lot—and he did everything big. Spend money, gamble, and invest. He put *big* in the term *Big shot*. Why the hell Travis was working for the BLM was a question everyone asked since Calvin liked to have everyone, including his son, under this thumb.

Travis always answered, "I want to make my own way, and I don't like the oil business."

If this were true, Bailey thought, he might not be the little prick I had always thought he was, but I doubt it.

As Knight was leaving he spotted Bailey and came over to his booth. "It looks like my boy might be taking over your job, I hear. Train him good, Bailey, he's going to be moving up to some high levels there. Hell, maybe even get all the way to Washington."

Bailey looked at him the same as when he stepped in some dog crap on the sidewalk. "No doubt, Calvin, no doubt."

Calvin clapped him on the back, gave a little chuckle and said as he left, "Maybe you can come work for me, Bailey, you know a lot about the country. Maybe you could ferret out some oil."

"Hell, Calvin, you never know." His appetite nearly gone, he ordered a salad and wondered if there was any justice for the sinner.

Chapter Eight

The initial part of the plan was simple. Drive to the Red Desert east of Rock Springs and they would kill some horses. As many as they could. They were to be met by a fella who would take them out into a remote area of the desert. Then they'd drive to Rawlins and hole up in a motel until they were ready to begin their second act.

Streck had three AR-15s courtesy of Tommy "The Blade". He had hidden them in the trunk of Patsy Mae's Buick. If any of them were to be stopped by the cops and a search done, nothing would point to Streck if the rifles were found. He would never be in the same car with the other two, at least until they started the job; nor would he be in very close proximity while traveling. The AR-15s had been picked because Streck felt in order to do a job right, you needed the correct tools.

They reached Rock Springs around three Wednesday afternoon and drove to the Coal Miner Motel, on Elk Street.

"For the room and food." Streck handed Lynch $100 in twenties before he went into the motel office. "I'll be on the first floor, room 113." Streck told them when he came out, a key in his hand.

"Tell the woman you want upstairs. Call me when you're in your room." Streck drove his car around to the back then walked to his room. He closed the door, went to the phone, and dialed a local number.

"Miner's Bar and Grill, can I help you?" The voice over the phone was a pleasant sounding female's.

"I need to talk to Jamie, please." Streck wasn't used to being decent over the phone, but he didn't know Jamie's last name; he had been told to get him through the bar.

"He's here, hold on for a minute." She must have let the phone hang because he could hear it bouncing off the wall.

The phone was picked up and cautiously answered with a hello.

"This is Streck; we're supposed to get a little guide service from you." Streck didn't like depending on someone he didn't know. Who knew where their loyalties were? A guy had to be sure there wouldn't be any squealing to the cops.

"Yeah, that's right. I wasn't expecting you until later tonight. We'll meet at Denny's in the morning, 'bout seven. It's right off Delmar and I-80. Where you at? I'll tell you how to get there."

"It ain't none of your concern, I can find it. You need to have something on so I'll know you."

"I'll be in the smoking side, to the right when you walk in, I'll have a brown work jacket and a red neckerchief on."

Streck told him they'd meet him, then hung up the phone and called Lynch's room. When Lynch answered, he said,

"We're meeting in the morning. We'll go out, do the job, then head to Rawlins. Stick around here and don't drive around. Get a bottle or something to keep you happy for the rest of the night. We can eat in the café here and I saw a liquor store across the street."

Lynch agreed, telling him to call them in the morning when he got up. Streck hung up the phone. He went over to the liquor store and bought a pint of Old Crow and a six-pack of Sheridan beer. He threw some pickled eggs and a box of smoked beer sausage into the sack then paid for it all and went back to his room to wait out the night.

Thursday morning, KCNC News: "The body of a young middle-aged woman was found early this morning in a field west of Sixth Avenue and C-470. She was found without any identification.

The police are currently investigating this as a homicide. More details will be coming after the police identify the young lady and the next of kin are notified."

Streck turned the TV off and called Lynch to get them up. Then he looked in the phone book for the local map and located Delmar Street and I-80.

They drove up in separate cars; Streck went in first and saw Jamie, sitting down across from him. Lynch and Gomez came in and sat in the booth behind Jamie.

Jamie looked Streck over, frown lines evident on his face.

"I thought we would drive down to Point of Rocks, you guys can leave your cars there and we'll take my Explorer. We're going to need a four-wheel drive to get where we're going."

They ate breakfast and the three vehicles left the parking lot heading east on I-80.

They came to Point of Rocks after a drive of twenty minutes and pulled into the rest area. A hundred yards down was a café and gas station doing a booming breakfast trade. No one else was parked where they were. Streck told Lynch to open the trunk of the Buick, and then he leaned in and emerged from it carrying a blanket wrapped around the rifles. Lynch and Gomez just watched, oblivious to the fact they were carrying rifles that would have put them in Federal prison if the serial numbers were ever checked.

Streck put the blanket in the back of the Explorer and got in the front passenger side. Lynch and Gomez climbed into the back seat. Jamie put the outfit into drive and drove back onto the Interstate.

"It'll take us about an hour to get there. You know I'm not doing anything except driving? You also know no one wants me messed with?"

Streck nodded his head and kept looking down the road.

In just a little over an hour with most of the driving on a dirt road, they came up on a herd of horses down in a draw where wild grass started to grow and water ran into a small watering hole. They were downwind. Jamie had them get out and low crawl fifty feet up to the top of the draw. The rifles were loaded and each had a spare clip. Streck told them when he gave the signal to fire as fast as they could. They got into position, the horses unaware.

"Shoot!" And they did. The gunfire rang out, almost a continual staccato sound. Horses dropped, cried out, and ran. When the carnage was over, twenty-three horses were lying dead in the draw. Jamie had known what was going to happen but the big guy, Streck, the crazy fucker had a huge smile on his face. Then Streck slowly turned to face Jamie leveling the rifle at his gut.

Jamie froze. "Oh no! Please, don't kill me. No one's supposed to fuck with me."

"I don't need to tell you to keep your mouth shut. These horses aren't found in a week, you call anonymously, right?"

"Christ, yes! You don't need to worry! I've been told nothing except what I told you." His voice was quavering. "I just want to take you guys back then forget everything."

When they pulled up to the cars at the rest area, Jamie stared straight ahead, not saying anything as Streck put the guns back into the trunk of the Buick.

"See ya, kid, it's been fun," Streck said.

Jamie slammed the Explorer into gear and squealed out of the lot, heading back to Rock Springs for an early drink.

"You smell the little prick? Lynch laughed. "He shit his pants."

    *   *   *   *   *   *   *   *   *

The two cars stopped at Wamsutter to gas up. Streck stuck his head into the other car. "We're gonna split up here. You guys stay at the Sunset Motel; it's right on the main drag. Check in under the name of Pittman. I'll call you in a day or two. Now listen — don't get stoned or in any kind of trouble. Do your drinking at the motel and there are some cafes around where you can eat. You don't need to drive around." Streck withdrew his head, then stuck it back in the car window.

"Any questions?"

"What about the guns? You want us to clean 'em?"

"No, just leave them in the trunk; I got them hid pretty good." Streck fired the Pontiac up and drove onto the eastbound exit and headed to Rawlins.

He took the by-pass around town and came in from the east side. He drove up Cedar Street and meandered with the main drag as it turned north, then west onto Spruce Street.

Carefully observing the motel parking lots, he was looking for one with a lot of cars parked out front, lot of business. The more cars, the less his would be noticed. He stopped near the edge of town at the Cottentree Inn. He put a neckerchief around his neck to hide his tattoo, and walked in to the desk and got a room.

"All right, Mr. Logan, your cost will be $42.50 a night. Will this be charge?" The young bright-eyed desk clerk looked like she really gave a crap. He was impressed.

"No, I'll pay cash. You do accept cash, don't you?" He said it with a smile cracking the sides of his mouth.

"Of course we do. I'm sorry, people don't usually pay by cash." She had giggled a little after the explanation.

His eyes turned hard with a mean little glint.

"My credit cards were stolen the other day when I was staying down-town at another motel, that's why I'm checking in here. Hopefully you don't have any smart-assed thieves hanging around,"Streck said.

Her face paled and she stepped back a bit, "Oh, no sir, and I apologize if I said anything offensive." She looked in the direction of the manager's office.

Grabbing his key he looked her in the eyes again, "Nope, everything is just fine, little girl."

He went to his car and got his bag out, then went into his room and dialed a number on the phone.

"Hello," after three rings.

"This is Streck. I'm going need some directions to get out there." The conversation lasted twenty minutes with Streck asking a few questions and writing down a make-do map on the stationery the motel so conveniently furnished with a pen.

The next morning Streck's eyes slowly opened and peered at the empty bottle of Old Crow. His tongue was coated with a half inch of what had to be mouse shit. His lips were stuck closed and he'd drooled on the bed. Just another night in Paradise, he thought, as the beginnings of a headache started. He went to the bathroom where he pissed, then took four aspirin. It seemed like an effort to pick the phone up and call Lynch, who had answered the phone, "Mr. Pittman and his punk Gomez, may I help you?"

Streck heard Gomez tell Lynch to go fuck himself.

"If you guys are finished with each other, I'm gonna tell you what we're gonna do. You pick me up at the Cottontree Inn by the east side door at 5:00 a.m. tomorrow morning. We're going to go have some fun." Lynch started to say something, but Streck hung the phone up.

He spent the rest of the day driving around the town. He saw the brown hills without any trees on them, and stores downtown closed up. There had been a south wind blowing since he'd come into town. It blew down the streets, picking up paper and trash, then it would seem to pick up force and throw everything into the sky. Streck would have sworn it would have to stop, take a breath, but it didn't. It just kept on a-howling. Tommy had told him Rawlins had one of the higher rates of divorce and suicide per capita and the cause was supposed to be from the never-ending wind. Streck could believe it. He didn't like the town already and he'd only been there eighteen hours.

He saw the Golden Eagle Gas and Exploration Company sitting by itself east of town a bit. He wondered what the owner had gotten himself involved with to warrant what they were doing now, and were going to do. Streck thought this little project was going to have some killing in it, and not just horses.

5:00 a.m., Streck walked out of the east door of the motel and got into the Buick idling by the side of the curb. Lynch and Gomez were in the front with a bag of donuts and three big cups of coffee. Streck sat down in the back seat and Lynch handed him a cup and the bag. When he muttered thanks, both Lynch and Gomez raised their eyes in astonishment. Between bites Streck gave directions on getting out of town. They eventually pulled on to Highway 287 and were on their way to the horse refuge.

They got to Lamont about 5:45 a.m. and Streck told them to pull into the parking lot at Grandma's Café, over by the crew cab Ford pickup. No one else was around; the hood on the Ford was still warm but whoever had brought it out had left. Streck took a screwdriver from his coat and took the license plates off the Buick, then put them in the back seat of the truck.

"What's going on?" Gomez asked. Both he and Lynch were watching Streck as he took the guns and ammunition out of the trunk and put them under the truck's back seat.

"We're swapping outfits. We need a truck and Patsy Mae might be getting pissed about her car being gone so long, wherever she is. Don't want any cops checking the tags."

Streck had been told the truck had local plates stolen from a wrecked Cheyenne Oil Services truck parked in an old wrecking yard in town. This truck looked like an old Golden Eagle truck, with no name on it, of course, but the white and brown Ford had a good motor and drive-train. Streck got the keys from under the floor mat and the three took off north.

When Streck turned to the south at the abandoned oil recovery tank, he saw a dilapidated red Jeep parked along the road. There was an old dirty-looking bum standing over a clump of sagebrush pissing. When the bum heard the truck pull up, he zipped his pants up, squinting at them from under the bill of his hat. Streck stopped by the Jeep and got out. The old man limped over to where Streck was standing by the truck.

"You Logan?"

"Yeah, you Frank?"

"Yep, you're supposed to give me $500 in cash before we go any further." He licked his fingers, hardly able to wait to count the money.

Streck counted out five one hundred-dollar bills and put them in Frank's hand. "Let's get this going. We don't want to be out here all fucking day."

"You betcha," Frank replied. "The BLM guy who started this refuge is gonna be really pissed if he ever finds out. And he's a mean stud, so I don't wanna be here if he'd come out."

"You just remember, old man, you keep your mouth shut and no one will be any wiser."

They drove down rough dirt roads for better than an hour, following the old smoking Jeep when it suddenly turned up a draw and stopped. Frank got out and came back to the truck.

"I seen some tracks going below that ridge. If you climb up there they might be down below." He was sounding a little nervous and he kept licking his lips.

Streck, Lynch and Gomez got out of the truck, then pulled the rifles out and headed up the ridge.

Frank went back to the Jeep. "I think there's going to be hell to pay", he muttered.

The stallion heard something...

Chapter Nine

Saturday morning Bailey dialed Carl Toomes' number.

Carl answered with a gravelly and coarse voice. Too many cigarettes and cancer was probably peeking its ugly head out in the future.

"Carl, this is Bailey. How 'bout taking me up today for an hour or so?"

"Yeah, I could do it, Bailey. I got some things to do around the house, but I can meet you at the airport around ten this morning. Are you in a little better mood than the other night, cuz if you ain't, I ain't taking ya."

"Yeah, I'm in a hell of a lot better mood. I'll see you then, Carl." He gave a little prayer the wind would stay below 40 mph while they were in the air, but thought the odds were against it. Grabbing his binoculars and topo map, he fed the dog then jumped into his truck, driving to the airport to wait for Carl.

He pulled along side a small private hangar near the old control office. A short time later Carl arrived. He parked his car by Bailey's, pulled out a key and unlocked the padlock to the hangar door, then opened it.

"Bailey, gimme a hand and lift the rear of the plane up; we'll push it out of the hangar. You've done it before. She's a SuperCub and she's light."

Carl went into the office and filed a local flight plan, then the two pushed the plane over to the gas pump and filled the tanks. It was Bailey's turn to go into the office where he paid $56.00 for the aviation fuel. Carl was already in the cockpit when Bailey came out and climbed into the seat behind. The SuperCub was a 1955, with a beefed-up, 150-hp Lycombing engine Carl had put in one dark night in his hangar. A nice thing about Rawlins was having single hangars with power to them. For $125.00 a month, you could park your plane, store things or pretty well do what you wanted. Carl had taken the opportunity to put the different engine in without having to go through a FAA certified mechanic, saving himself $40.00 an hour. Bailey always hoped he had tightened the nuts and bolts right.

Carl fired the engine up and circled the plane to make sure there weren't any planes coming in, then headed down the runway. Reaching 70 mph, he pulled the stick back and lifted off.

The plane climbed to 4000 feet above elevation and banked to the north.

The cockpit noise was loud. Carl shouted, "What are we looking for, Bailey?" His gray hair, sticking out from under his hat, was blown back from a vent in the front of the plane where air flowed into the cockpit. He turned and looked at Bailey.

"I just want to scout the refuge area, Carl. I found some dead horses and I want to see if there's anymore. When we get out there, we'll just need enough height so we can see for some distance but be able to recognize anything down there. I'd like you to start around Riley's Ridge then grid it to the south."

"You got it, Bailey. We'll even bring her down if you want to be on the ground and look at something."

Shit, I hope we don't have to land. Bailey nodded his head and pulled his seat belt tighter.

They flew over Lamont and Bailey saw Grandma's Café down below. Looked like business was good. Also looked like the old Buick was still there. Minnie must have found her a man. Bailey smiled to himself as he envisioned Minnie having the guy locked in the back room.

They started a sweeping turn that took them close to the Ferris Mountains and looped them around to come in from the north. Carl dropped the Cub down to 2500 ft. and started making a grid.

Sighting the first group of dead horses he had seen, he motioned to Carl to start a circle then make it bigger. Fifteen minutes after they had started their search they crossed the old stage stop. They passed over a small box canyon and Bailey thought he spotted something. "Carl, drop her lower and slower if you can. I want to check out the stuff by the opening."

Carl pulled the flaps back and dropped into the canyon. Bailey thought his breakfast was going to come up so he started gulping to keep it down. Carl banked the plane side to side to get a view from the canyon opening to the end of it, which was a short ways past a watering hole to some outcroppings.

Scattered across the canyon floor near the opening, looking like the buffalo had after the hunters had gunned them down, were at least twenty horses.

Bailey yelled at Carl, "Any way we can land in there and still get out?"

Carl flew over the entrance to the canyon, mentally measuring the width of the opening. "Yeah——maybe. Hold on to your ass and we'll see." He pulled the flaps all the way down, raised the nose and floated in just after the opening and dropped it down. He pushed the toe brakes down as hard as he could and with a little sliding of the wheels, came to a stop.

"Hot damn! If the opening wouldn't have been angled going up the sides, I'd never of tried taking her in."

Bailey didn't think he could move. The canyon walls weren't tall, mostly outcroppings of rocks forming a bowl, but an animal like a horse or antelope wouldn't have been able to climb out. They would have had to go through the entrance. He didn't think the plane could have made it in, and he wasn't sure if it could make it out. He found he could move when he decided the hell with it — they'd make it out or wouldn't. He unbuckled his seat belt and climbed out the side.

Walking over to the entrance first, he saw a gate made up of brush and a few limbs from some scrub cedar. It was lying next to one of the walls and there were some large rocks used to brace it against the sides of the opening when the gate was closed. The gate was primitive but effective. Turning, he started walking towards the dead horses, and he felt a fear rising in him that the buckskin would be one of the dead horses. Carl was silent, the incredulous look on his face telling his emotions.

"Carl, see if there's a buckskin stallion here." His voice cracked a little.

They searched through the dead horses, some were on top of others and some were away from the group. The stallion was found down by the watering hole. "Here's the stallion, Bailey, but it's a bay. He's old enough; this is his herd."

Relief flooded through him, knowing the buckskin wasn't here. All the herds ranged from fifteen to forty horses. Any more and the younger studs came in and took several mares to start their own harems. The bigger herds meant the stallion was in his fighting prime and able to keep them together. The buckskin was one of those in their prime.

Bailey was astounded someone could have killed an entire herd of horses. This was a hell of lot more than some gun-nut crazies running around. Something was happening and Bailey was going to find out.

Carl asked Bailey if he wanted to bust the gate up or burn it. Keep whoever from using it again.

"There's one other canyon like this and if it happens again, they might want to use it so let's bust it up. Won't be any horses coming in here with all the death around. I want to dig some bullets out and check the top of the canyon for casings.

Give me a hand, will you?" Bailey asked. They grabbed the makeshift fence and broke it into small pieces, then scattered them into the wind.

Both of them had been gagging from the smell, but they were able to recover about two dozen intact bullets. Bailey climbed the south side of the bowl, and after walking towards the east, found casings strewn on the ground like fallen leaves.

They must have shot over 60 rounds. He gathered them into a large plastic baggy he had pulled out of his shirt then carefully negotiated his way to the canyon floor. "Let's get out of here if we can, Carl, I'm about ready to puke from the smell." He didn't tell Carl, but he also had a psycho feeling in his gut. An overbearing urge for justice, not the law. And justice for Bailey included a cleansing.

They climbed back into the plane, Bailey strapping himself in as tight as the seat belt would go. The engine roared to life and the plane shook as Carl steered it as far back from the entrance as he could get, then he turned and smiled at Bailey.

"The flaps are full down; don't say anything to me because I'm going to be concentrating on getting this up. OKAY?"

Bailey nodded his head and wondered how it would feel to smack into the top of the entrance.

Carl pushed the throttle to the end of the slide and held the brakes. The Cub screamed and bucked then he let it go. They started off slow, Bailey thought too slow, then picked up speed. The entrance was coming faster towards them; Carl had the tail up. Just as they came into the shadow of the opening, Carl yanked the nose up. They bounced into the air like a basketball over the entrance, then he dropped the nose to pick up air speed and Bailey thought they were screwed forever. *Yea, tho' I walk through the Valley of Death.* Carl yanked the nose up again and the plane settled in at 70 feet off the ground, heading south.

"Jesus Christ, Carl! I thought we'd had it."

"Bailey, you're turning into a big puss." The smile was broad across his face, but a few drops of sweat could be seen on his forehead.

They started climbing and turning over the canyon. Carl banked to the west and they flew over the base of Green Mountain. Bailey saw Frank's shack and the red Jeep sitting in front of it. He asked Carl to fly south, over the other box canyon. It was similar to the one they had just left except there was a road to the top and the entrance was smaller. It looked more like a natural corral than a canyon. Not deep, but able to hold some horses in it. There would be no landing in that one. For Bailey there wouldn't be anymore landings until the airport.

Carl dropped her low when they came to the canyon, but there wasn't anything that looked out of the ordinary. He took it back up to 4500 feet and inside of a half-hour they were landing at the airport. Fortunately it had been one of those rare days when the wind hadn't blown much. Apparently the weather report Bailey had listened to the day before had been wrong.

Bailey climbed out and helped Carl wheel the plane back into the hangar. "Thanks, Carl, but do me a favor, don't mention this to anyone."

"Don't worry, I won't say anything, but I want you to get those bastards, Bailey."

"It's coming — thanks again." Shaking his hand, Bailey walked to his truck and drove home.

*   *   *   *   *   *   *   *   *

Bailey spent the night writing a report on the horses and starting a log of daily activities. This was a beerless night again for him and he was surprised to think of the nights gone by that he hadn't drunk any. He was anxious to talk to Deputy Maes in the morning to see if there were any similarities in the killings. He had a sack full of spent cartridges and bullets he wanted to send to Maes if he'd take them, and have ballistics run on them to see if they matched. Bailey wasn't sure if the Rock Springs S. O. would send them to Cheyenne to the Criminal Division of the Attorney General's Office, or if they had the ability to do their own ballistics. Hoping they could do their own, Bailey packed them in a box ready to ship. All he would have to do is put a letter in before he taped it shut.

Chapter Ten

The first thing he heard when he woke up was the wind. It was howling out of the north and when it would gust, it made a piece of metal trim on the house vibrate, sounding like an off-tune violin doing measures. He got out of bed and opened the shade covering the window. Clouds were rolling in looking like dark ocean waves breaking on a pier. They were dirty gray and ominous looking. It looked like an early spring snow was in the making. *It was amazing; 6:00 a.m. and the damn wind is trying to blow the house down already. Unfucking believable.*

He could gaze out over most of the town because his house was located in a section where it was elevated a bit. He saw the streetlights start to blink out and was able to see porch lights still on, waiting for the shift workers to come home.

This was a town he had lived in most of his life, yet he seemed to bitch and moan about it constantly the last couple of years.

For all the shortcomings of the town its greatest asset was the people.

Dana used to tell him, "One thing I'll say about Rawlins, you can go to the grocery store or the post office and always have someone say hello to you. Not a time goes by that you don't see someone you know. They don't have this in Denver."

Bailey had to agree with her. The people were friendly, community-minded and trying to upgrade the town. It was a railroad town, built along the U.P. line back in the late 1800's.

In the summer the temperatures were in the high 80's and the nights mid to low 50's. Looking to the east one would see a magnificent view of Elk Mountain and the Snowy Range. To the north the Ferris Mountains; their rich hue of blue and granite stood out from the horizon looking like a slumbering dinosaur.

You couldn't beat the summers. But the damn wind. It seemed to blow most of the winter, spring and three fourths of the summer. The times it didn't blow there was a collective sigh and the lowering of shoulders. Normally most people ached from hunching against the wind all the time.

Bailey was surprised he had slept so well the past night. Usually he would lie in bed tossing and turning, thinking about the job or Dana or getting older, then just as he would be ready to doze off, he'd have to get up and piss. He knew the last couple of nights that he had slept well was from not drinking any beer. A revelation: Don't drink beer if you want to sleep through the night.

Travis saying the horses he found were winterkilled bothered him quite a bit. It ate at him. It could be true, if winter slaughtered the horses with a rifle. He was going to talk to Travis after he found more information. With Williams being his nemesis, Bailey knew he would have to walk very softly and have indisputable facts.

He was the first to arrive in the office that morning. Usually around 7:45 a.m., everyone started traipsing in. Bailey had almost an hour to himself. He picked up the telephone and called the Rock Springs Sheriff's Office. Being told Deputy Maes wouldn't be in until eight, Bailey left his number and asked for a message to be left requesting that Maes call him. He looked around and went over to Travis's desk, not touching anything, just looking at the mess on the top. *Jesus, I could throw half this crap away and he'd never know it.* Moving a paper or two very carefully Bailey saw a note Travis had written to himself. "Check Frank/red jeep/plates?" He eased the papers

74

back the way they had seemed then went over to William's office. Turning the doorknob and trying to push the door open, he found it was locked.

Shit, wouldn't you know he'd lock his damn door. Bailey went over and started the coffee machine when Williams walked in, giving Bailey a start.

"Here a little early, aren't you, Bailey?" Unlocking his door he put his coat and hat on a hook inside his office.

"Yeah, I thought I would get an early start on the rancher's lease renewal proposals and waivers."

"Good! I'm glad to see you're taking more of an active interest in the management part of this department." Williams poured himself a cup of coffee then went into his office, closing his door behind him.

He usually never closed his door unless he was talking with someone or was going to be on the phone a long time. Everyone knew when he closed it he didn't want to be disturbed. Bailey saw through the glass window in the door Williams took some papers out of his briefcase and appeared to be studying them.

Dora came in at exactly 8:00 a.m. She went to the coffee machine, got herself a cup, one container of cream, one teaspoon of sugar, stirred it four times, then walked over to her desk. Opening the bottom drawer she shoved her purse in it then hung her coat up on the rack by the main door. She looked the entire room over, making sure her fiefdom was presentable and everybody accountable. Two sips of coffee and she turned her computer on then began typing on it with the speed of a typist attempting to set a new land speed record.

Bailey walked over to her desk and asked, "Where's Travis signed out for today, Dora?" Swearing she was typing with one hand, she opened a logbook with the other, turning a page and running her finger down the lines.

"It looks like he's out in the field this week, Bailey. He's scheduled to meet with some lease applicants in Rock River Wednesday. He'll be back in the office Thursday."

"What's John got going? He usually doesn't isolate himself in his office that way." The windows made small pinging noises as the first snowflakes started hitting them.

Looking around then lowering her voice she said, "He's been doing some research the last couple of days for Mr. Knight. He hasn't had me do anything and he takes his papers home so I don't know what he's checking." She returned to her rapid-fire typing.

Thanking her, Bailey went back and sat down at this desk. He pulled the lease proposals out of his drawer and reluctantly began going through them. The stack was fairly high and Bailey thought if Dennis would have been in a little bit better shape, he wouldn't have had the heart attack, thereby not retiring early, therefore Dennis would be doing the boring shit.

Maybe that's why he had it, to get out of doing this crap. He looked out the window and saw the slate-colored sky still teasing by dropping some more of the light snow.

Looking down at the papers, he saw buried in the stack an application for a proposal to drill exploratory gas wells beginning June first of this year. The land description encompassed the horse refuge, and the applicant was Golden Eagle Gas and Exploration. *What the hell is going on here? I haven't heard anything about this.* The filing date had been six weeks ago. He was rudely brought back from his pondering by the ringing of his telephone. Answering it he heard Deputy Maes from the Rock Springs Sheriff's Office say, "Mr. Calhoun, I understand you wanted to talk to me about the wild horse killings a couple of weeks ago? What would you like to know? And please, call me Rudy."

"Okey, Rudy, I'm Bailey. I came across two different groups of wild horses killed out on our refuge. Fifteen in the first bunch and twenty in the second. We recovered quite a few bullets and casings and I was wondering if you guys had gotten any from your investigation."

"Yeah, we got about two dozen bullets from the horses. Picked up a crap load full of casings also. They were .223 caliber and the casings are standard. Bailey, you have to understand we can't pin down when it exactly happened. They'd been dead for a while and if we hadn't received an anonymous phone call telling us where to find them, God only knows when we would have found out about it. One thing's for certain, though; whoever did it are a bunch of cold-blooded bastards."

"Rudy, if I send you the bullets and casings I recovered, can you guys

76

run some ballistics and see if any match? The ones I got are .223 also. I don't believe in that kind of coincidence."

Maes' voice coming over the telephone sounded more alert and a little more intense. "You bet! Get them down here and I'll have our lab check your bullets against ours. You might be on to something, Bailey. Listen, I want you to keep me informed and updated on this. This really pissed me off when I saw those horses. Christ, they killed mares, colts; they didn't seem to give a shit what they killed. And they weren't all clean hits."

"You got it. Give me a number I can get in touch with you without having to go through the S.O. And thanks. I'll get the bullets out today." He wrote the numbers down for Maes's cell and home telephone, then stuck his cover letter into the package. He taped it and got his coat on, yelling to Dora as he went out the door, "I'll be back in twenty minutes, got a package I've got to mail."

Williams watched him as he left.

The wind had picked up and the snow came down in icy hard sheets that stung when they hit. Bailey turned his collar up and lowered his head as he was pushed by the wind at his back to the post office.

He went in and mailed the package then stood at the entrance deciding what to do. Travis was gone for the better part of the week; Williams had something going on with Knight and wasn't coming out of his office and he would have to wait for news on the bullets. He decided he'd walk up to the library and talk to Dana. She would be polite and courteous because she didn't like scenes in public. They had never had a harsh or loud word anywhere except when they were by themselves.

He struck out in the storm like Moses leading the way. By the time he arrived at the library his hair and coat were a sheet of white. The snow had picked up strength and Bailey was silently cursing himself for not driving the four blocks. He was cold and wet and the snow was melting as he climbed the stairs.

It was running down the back of his neck in ice-cold rivulets that made him shiver. He walked up to Dana's desk and stood in front of it until she looked up at him. She burst out laughing, "Bailey, you look like Callie dragged you through a snow bank." His wet hair was hanging straight down by then and his face had one of those woe-begotten looks she loved so much.

"Dana, if you aren't busy right now, how about going and having a cup of coffee with me? I want to visit about some things going on and I'm not quite sure what to make of it."

Standing up she reached for her coat. "Okay, Bailey. I could use a cup and a little intrigue."

With the usual early spring weather, the sun had started to break out from the clouds. Of course the wind still blew with enough chill that Dana's cheeks were a bright red when they got to the Square Shooters Restaurant. A booth in the back was available when they entered and after ordering donuts and coffee, Bailey took one of her hands into his.

"I've really missed you. I'm not going to push, but I want you to know I'm going to change for you. You don't need to say anything now, but just so you know."

Her eyes filled with tears; she didn't speak but held his hand tighter. "What's going on at work, Bailey? You're acting a little anxious," she said after a moment.

He started telling her how he had discovered the dead horses on Saturday and more on Sunday. He paused while the waitress served their coffee and donuts, then picked up with his story after she left.

"This morning I was going through some lease proposals and came across one from Golden Eagle submitted about six weeks ago. The area they applied for is the refuge. Now why the hell would they put in for an area that's a horse refuge? There's no way it could happen. And to top it off, Williams is doing something for Knight, but no one has any idea what." The frustration in his voice was evident.

"I can see how maddening this must be for you," Dana responded in a low soft voice. "I think you need to wait until Travis comes back first and ask him about the horses you found shot. There must be an explanation why he said they were winterkilled. Though I must admit it sounds very strange. Remember, Bailey, your virtue has never been patience, so try not running off half-cocked."

"I think you're right, Dana. I'm going to snoop around a little and I'll

78

wait until Travis gets back and talk to him. Hey, maybe I'll talk to Dennis and see what he thinks."

"That would be a good idea; if nothing else he'll keep you from jumping to conclusions. Listen, why don't you come over for dinner tonight? About seven. Jennie will be at a church service so you won't have to contend with hearing about what kind of a heathen you are." She put her hand over her mouth to cover the smile on her lips.

"I'd like that, Dana. I'm probably just getting paranoid. At least I know now you aren't out to get me." They both grinned at his joke as they left to go back to the library. Bailey took her to the research desk, put his finger to his lips and placed it on her forehead.

"I'll see you tonight," he said.

Taking the stairs instead of the elevator, he seemed to have a little bounce in his step and he felt like doing a little jig to his desk. He sat down and looked at the lease proposals. Something didn't look right; the proposal from Golden Eagle wasn't there. He rummaged through all the proposals, but it was definitely gone. Looking over at Williams's office it was apparent he had left. No hat or coat on the hook, his briefcase gone and desktop neat, nothing out of place. Bailey saw Dora still typing—probably a 1000 words a minute. There was an eerie silence hanging in the air; he couldn't hear either her keyboard being banged on by both hands or the tune she was whistling to herself. He ambled over to Williams's office and opened the door. His neck flushed and it felt like the temperature had risen 90 degrees as he glided over to the desk.

"What do you need, Bailey?" He almost jumped. He turned around to see her looking at him, her eyes blazing with indignity.

"I'm missing a lease proposal. It was sitting on my desk when I left earlier. I thought maybe John had taken it."

She sniffed and seemed to be looking down her nose at him (anyone who screwed with Williams or his stuff, screwed with her).

"I saw him pick up some papers from your desk, but I haven't any idea what they were. I think you might want to ask him rather than go through his things."

"For Christ's sake, Dora, I wasn't going through his things; I was look-ing to see if they were on top of his desk." He walked out of Williams's office and returned to his desk, sitting down with a big sigh.

"Bailey Calhoun, I don't appreciate you using the Lord's name in vain." She'd walked over to his desk, hands on her hips.

"I apologize, Dora, I certainly didn't mean to offend you, really." He put some extra whine into it and it seemed to help.

She seemed mollified with his apology and murmured for him to leave it as it was. Please, no more, you may rise from your knees, was the look she gave him.

Fortunately, the day ended without any confrontations. Williams didn't come back to the office and Dora kept to herself. He left at 4:00 p.m. antici-pating the night. The bounce was back in his step.

Seven p.m. A freshly showered Bailey rang the doorbell and gave her the flowers when she opened the door. "Bailey, how nice. Come in, give me your coat." She took his coat and put it on the couch, then found a vase and gently put the flowers in it. "They are beautiful. You didn't need to, but I'm glad you did."

The dinner was a success. Bailey hoped Dana noticed he didn't have anything to drink except water.

This ought to surprise her, not drinking any beer.

"Bailey, you can have a beer if you like." She got up from the table. "I'm not a teetotaler, you know that; but it just seemed you started to drink more and more as your problems got bigger." Dana's voice quivered.

"We quit talking; it seemed like you would just bitch and moan and do nothing except get drunk for the last six months. But I'm proud of you; you're making an effort to change," she said.

"Sit back down, Dana, you're right, I just hadn't seen it. Until you left me."

With dinner over and Jenny expected back soon, Bailey got his coat and made ready to leave. Putting his arms around her he hugged her tight. "Come home with me, Dana, I really need you."

She pulled away from him, went to the table and wrote something down on a note pad, then took her coat from the closet and putting her arm through his, said, "Hell, I need you too, Bailey. Let's give her a shot." Laughing together, they left the house and went to their home.

Chapter Eleven

"All right, we'll get her done. Tomorrow if we can." Streck disconnected the call then dialed Lynch's room. "Pick me up in the morning at 5:00 a.m.; we're going back out." He hung up and laid down on the bed thinking how he was going to get some horses into a canyon. The first time was lucky. They were in the wash and shooting from the ridge made it pretty easy, but the ground was so rough out there off the road he knew they couldn't get them in with just the truck. If he had a saddle horse he could herd them down to the canyon and move them in with a little help from the truck. It would work if the horses were anywhere near the canyon. He didn't want to use the old bum again; Frank made him uneasy. In fact Streck thought the old man was going to cause some trouble, he was greedy. He wasn't yours when he was paid for. Streck lifted the telephone again and made his second call within ten minutes to the man.

"This is Streck. I'm gonna need some side help. Maybe someone who knows the area, but not the old fart. I also need a saddle horse. Yeah...a saddle horse. The best thing would be if the guy could ride. Also, I think we're gonna need to drive them into the canyon if we want to get very many of them." Streck nodded to himself, "Okay, 7:00 a.m., a half mile from the old oil tank." He mentally gave himself a pat on the back. This ought to work good. Get a lot of 'em this way. He pulled a half-pint of Old Crow from his bag and opened a beer. Sitting on the bed with the TV on, he sipped his whiskey and chased it with beer while he watched the news out of Denver.

"Good evening, this is Francine Brookman reporting for KCNC News. The body discovered last Thursday in the field west of 6th Street and C-470 has been identified as Patsy Mae Brinkman, 34 years of age, living in Denver. The victim had been strangled and sexually molested. She was listed in the police files as a prostitute working the Capital Hill area. The police report they have a suspect they are investigating, but have not made any arrests at the present time. This is Francine Brookman reporting for KCNC News."

Streck's muscles constricted when he heard the report. He was surprised they had I.D.'d her so fast. He thought by taking her purse and throwing it in the Platte River, it would be awhile before her prints or dental records would identify her. Streck hadn't believed her name was really Patsy Mae Brinkman. He just hadn't given a big enough shit to care. Streck didn't think the cops could connect him to her murder. He raised his glass in a toast to Patsy Mae. With the empty whiskey bottle on the floor and three beer bottles sitting on the bed table, he fell into a fitful sleep.

The early morning was cold with frost on the windows of the cars in the parking lot. The sky was overcast as the sun was rising in the east. Some clouds hung low but gave the appearance of breaking up as the day grew older.

Lynch and Gomez were waiting in the truck as Streck came out of the side entrance. Getting into the back he told them to wake him up when they got to the turn-off by the old oil tank. Looking at each other with raised eyebrows, Lynch turned the radio on to a country and western station, turning the volume up. There wasn't any conversation as the truck sped north. When they passed Lamont, Lynch woke Streck up by asking what he was going to do with the car that was still there. "I wouldn't mind having it if nobody hauls it off." Lynch was looking at it longingly as they drove by.

"Look, Lynch, it's been involved in some serious shit so you don't want to take a chance on being connected with it now. Cops catch you driving it and you might end up getting the needle for murder. You get my drift?"

Streck was staring at Lynch through the rear view mirror, his eyes hard and glinting.

"We got one, maybe two weeks more, tops, then we're out of here. You guy's will have about six grand each by then so you can buy you a better car than that piece of shit, and have some bucks left over. And who knows what other jobs will be coming up after we're done with this one." Streck stretched in the back seat and said, "Streck and Associates, no job too big or small. Sounds pretty impressive, huh?"

They turned at the oil tank and drove down the road coming upon a blue Chevy pickup with a two-horse trailer hooked to the back. Streck got out of their truck and walked over to the Chevy, getting in the passenger side.

Fritz Meade was a middle-aged rancher that had battled with the BLM and the state for several years regarding grazing rights. He thought he paid too much for land that was actually owned by the people. His mentality was similar to the *posse comitatus* radical group that had made the news in Montana. He wasn't the hard-working, respected rancher that fought the elements to scrape out a living because they loved the land.

Meade looked over at Streck when he closed the door.

"Streck? My name's Fritz Meade; we have a common connection who called me and said you needed a horse and some help. Got a couple of saddle horses in the back. He said something about the wild horses, so tell me what you got in mind."

"Okay, Meade. There's a box canyon west of an old stage stop. The land by the entrance is too rough to run horses into it by truck. If we can find some horses over by the canyon and kind of round them up and get them into the canyon, we'll be able to take care of the horses pretty easy from the top. Were you told what's gonna happen?"

Meade nodded his head. "I ain't got a problem with that. Those goddamn government people are keeping me off what's rightfully mine just so's they can have a refuge for wild horses." He snorted, "Christ, there's more wild horses than God knows what to do with in this state and they're protected anyway. Then they drink all the water and eat all the grass. Good riddance to them, I say. I know the canyon you're talking about. It'll take us about an hour or so to get there."

Streck told him he wanted to go to the canyon first and make up a brush gate so they could close it after they got the horses in. Then with the trucks acting as a chute, he and Meade would ride the saddle horses and maneuver the horses into the canyon where Lynch and Gomez would secure the gate.

The road was rough and some areas were washed out. Numerous times the Chevy and horse trailer scraped bottom and they rolled and swayed through the holes and washouts. They pulled up about a quarter-mile to the west of the canyon entrance where there were rolling hills and rock outcroppings leading into the canyon. They parked their trucks and walked to the front of the entrance while picking up brush and scrub cedar branches. They made up a makeshift gate and tied some red rags that Meade had brought with him.

"This will keep them away from the gate after it's closed. Lynch, you and Gomez tie some of the branches so they'll stick out into the entrance." Meade ordered.

"Who's that cowboy think he is? A screw? We got too many chiefs and only two Indians." Lynch whispered to Gomez as they started tying the branches.

"Hey man, I don't give a shit. Soon as this is over, I'm getting my money and heading back to Denver, do some partying." Gomez replied.

"Jesus, I haven't had any pussy or smoked any dope for a week."

When the fence was done they walked back to the truck and Meade opened the horse trailer door. Going inside he led out a chestnut mare that was already saddled and bridled. He lifted the stirrup and tightened up the cinch then swung into the saddle.

"You need me to saddle your horse for you, Streck?"

"Oh, I think I can handle it. I done some riding before."

"Fine, why don't you have your guys park the trucks in a line facing the canyon on the south side of the entrance. I'll go up here aways and try to round some up to get them going this way. When you see the herd, bust ass over and we'll drive them in, then Lynch and Gomez can close the gate. Put them rocks against it to hold it in place. Savvy?"

"Yeah, I got it. Now, you listen to me, you don't give me orders." Streck said over his shoulder as he was getting into Meade's truck. "You got that?"

"Yeah...yeah I got it. No offense, man."

"Come on, you guys, get in the Ford and drive it up to the left about fifty yards from the gate", Streck ordered. "I'll follow in the Chevy and pull in behind you about twenty yards."

Lynch raced the engine then popped the clutch. The Ford lurched forward in granny gear towards the canyon. Streck put the Chevy into low range and followed. The sagebrush crunched and rocks spit out as the tires clawed for traction. When they got into position Streck went into the horse trailer. He guided the horse out of the back and holding on to the halter, threw the blanket then the saddle on the horse's back, sliding it up to rest on the withers. Both Gomez and Lynch were watching with a surprised look on their faces as Streck knowingly stuck the bit in the horse's mouth. He had been raised on a farm in Nebraska; always being the first to *put 'em out of their misery* when an animal needed disposed of. His parents started worrying when the family pets began showing up dead.

All three looked up when they heard the sounds of the horses pounding up the shallow gullies running south, with Meade behind them swinging a bright scrap of rag in his hand. Streck pulled the cinch then kicked the horse in the stomach to blow the wind out and tightened the cinch up more as the horse stood shivering. He put his foot into the stirrup and swung into the saddle, then picking up the reins, he kicked the horse in the ribs and took off at a dead run toward the herd of horses.

He came in at an angle and together with Meade, they drove the horses into the box canyon. The canyon itself was fairly flat inside with a watering hole down towards the middle. Grass was growing and there was still snow lying in the shadows of the rocks.

Lynch and Gomez closed the gate then opened it enough for Meade and Streck to maneuver their horses out. They rode over to the trailer and dropped out of the saddles.

"Damn, that was good," Meade said as he loosened the cinch and took the bit out of the chestnut's mouth. "A man needs to come out and run those horses once in a while."

Streck did the same with the bit and saddle then led his horse into the back of the trailer. "You can leave now, Meade. We got her under control."

"I kind of thought I'd stay if you don't mind, see how you do it."

"No, you better go. No witnesses. You don't wanna be involved any-more than what you are already, so hop in your truck and cut out." Streck turned on his heel leaving Meade looking at his back as he walked over to the Ford and got in. Streck heard the Chevy start and pull out. Streck had the truck going when Lynch and Gomez bailed in, closing the door.

"What now, Kemosabe?" Gomez smiled with the big white teeth.

"We'll drive up as far as we can then climb to the top and do our thing. It'll also give them a chance to settle down a little, bunch up. That way we ought to be able to get them all." Streck's eyes had a glassy look in them and he seemed to be savoring the moment coming.

Chapter Twelve

When Bailey woke up the next morning with Dana at his side, he couldn't help the big smile that spread across his face. She lifted her head to him and puckered her lips.

"Gimme a kiss, big boy."

"Jesus, Dana, much as I love you I can't kiss someone whose breath smells like that." He rolled out of the bed and ran to the bathroom.

Dana heard the shower start and yelled to him,

"Don't take all the hot water."

It was so easy to fall back into the routine. She knew she wouldn't leave him permanently, but she wondered if they were going to slide back into the same old pattern. Quit trying to predetermine everything, she thought. If it works now, great. If not, then worry about it later. She agreed to herself that if he asked her to move back she would, and as Doris Day had once said, "Que sera, sera."

They had a pleasant breakfast together, making small talk, with just a little mystery in the air concerning their future.

"Dana, I want you to stay, but I think it would be better if you go back to Jenny's for a little while until you're sure. When you're ready, I'll be waiting with open arms."

She almost cried knowing that this was hurting him, but she loved him for giving her the opportunity to work it out without a deadline or ultimatum.

"You're right, Bailey, and it won't be long, I promise."

He dropped her off at Jenny's house and with a promise to call, he left for the office.

With coffee steaming in a cup, he settled down at his desk with the lease proposals in front of him. Before he talked to Williams about the missing sheets he was going to go through the whole stack to make sure he hadn't missed them.

Williams was in his office already with his door closed, going over some papers. *I wonder if that's the Golden Dick's proposal*, Bailey thought as he sipped his coffee. It took him well over an hour to sort through the lease agreements, waivers and proposals for future land use requests. He didn't find the proposal from the Golden Eagle so he knew it was time to talk to Williams. The only reason he didn't right then was the thought of calling Dennis and trying to get together with him. Like Dana said, "Don't go off half cocked, Bailey."

For once in his life instead of jumping into a situation with both feet, he was going to sit back and try to use a little common sense. He also wanted to talk to Travis when he got back about the horses he said he had found. Bailey had pulled Travis's form on the horses' deaths from the "to be filed" box and saw the stated cause of death was winterkill and the number of dead horses was twelve.

He tried putting together the information and suppositions in his mind, to see if he could get a handle on what or what he thought, was going on.

The first indication something was wrong was when Travis had said he found some horses that were winterkilled—they were shot and there were fifteen, not twelve.

The second thing was finding twenty horses killed in the box canyon—all shot; in fact both groups were killed with .223 caliber bullets.

The third indication, twenty-three horses killed in the Red Desert prior to his find and they were killed with .223 bullets.

The fourth was a fact—finding a lease proposal from the Golden Eagle for gas exploration on the refuge. Dated six weeks ago.

Fifth thing, indication and fact—Williams took the proposal from the desk and had been in some intense telephone conversations with Calvin Knight, father of Travis and owner of the Golden Eagle.

Bailey pulled his computer keyboard closer to him and made a file up, then he typed down all the information he knew up to that time. He put it in the file, then made himself a floppy disk of the file so he could take it home and work on it or send it to someone else.

Williams came over to Bailey's desk and laid a form down in front of him.

"Bailey, here's a travel voucher for you. I want you to go to Denver this Thursday and attend a seminar on Congressional Hearings on Land Management. It should be quite interesting and it will have an impact on the smaller regional offices like ours. We might end up fighting to keep our region from merging with the one in Fremont County."

He looked at Bailey thoughtfully.

"We're going to have to go over these lease proposals again, there seem to be some questionable proposals ready for submission."

Bailey straightened up and returned Williams's look.

"What do you mean 'questionable', John? We can discuss it now if you like, I wanted to visit with you anyway." *Slow down, remember, don't go off half-cocked.*

"No, I think when you get back from Denver will be soon enough." Williams said. "There's so many proposals with small errors, wrong dates and lacking signatures that we'll be spending several hours on them. We'll just wait until you get back." Williams turned away and started back to his office then looked at Bailey.

"You'll need to get the papers in today, Why don't you go down a day early? Give yourself a break, you need it." Williams went into his office and closed his door.

I probably shouldn't, but screw it; I'm going go down early and do some visiting, he thought.

Bailey retrieved his notebook that contained his phone numbers of associates and friends. Usually the numbers enabled him to by-pass the switchboards and receptionists. He saw the number he wanted and started dialing. Unfortunately this number went to the switchboard.

"United States Secret Service, may I help you?"

"Yes, this is Bailey Calhoun with the BLM side of our big happy family, is Special Agent Hampston in?"

Saying she'd check after qualifying the big happy family remark, she came back on and said he was on another line. Would he like to hold or leave a message?

Bailey told her he'd hold for a little bit then put his telephone on the speaker so he could keep looking through the pile of forms in front of him.

"This is Special Agent Hampston, how can I be of service to my old buddy and drinking pal?" The speaker was loud and everyone looked over at Bailey who turned red and fumbled for the handset.

Mike Hampston and Bailey had roomed together for two years at the University in Laramie. When Bailey had ended up with the police department in Rawlins, Mike had joined the Highway Patrol then had eventually been recruited by the local Secret Service agent in Cheyenne. He had traveled around, being stationed in different cities over the years; and finally winding up in Denver as a Special Agent. Bailey and he would get together when one or the other would come to their respective towns to bullshit and party.

"Mike, I'm going to be in Denver day after tomorrow for a quote, 'interesting seminar' unquote, and I'm going to stay over through Friday. Can we have lunch Thursday?"

"Hey, you bet, Bailey. You buying?"

"Sure, I'll treat you to a big Irish lunch at Duffy's. The Bureau of Land Management will be pleased to pick the tab up. Duffy's is still on Sixteenth and Court Place, isn't it? Or has someone torn it down to put another boutique in to serve the prominent and affluent of the city like yourself?"

"No, some things we leave alone. There's too many Irish in the city to let anybody try to get rid of it." Hampston laughed.

"Okay, I'll come by around 11:30 a.m.. If something comes up, and you can't make it, give me a call." Bailey said.

"Unless someone drops some funny money downstairs, there shouldn't be a problem. Is Dana coming with you?"

"No, she's working, but she says hello."

Mike was a confirmed bachelor, but he always sounded sincere when asking about Dana. *The bastard's probably hitting on her*. He chuckled a little to himself after hanging the phone up and put the floppy disk in his pocket.

Dora came over. "John already told me you were going to the seminar, Bailey, so you're booked at the Downtown Comfort Suites. The seminar is across the street in the Brown Palace conference room. It starts at 1:00 p.m. and goes until 6:00, then begins at 9:00 a.m. Friday morning and finishes at five. Here's your confirmation numbers." She gave him the slip of papersand seminar information sheet.

"Thanks Dora, I think I'll go down Wednesday night, too late to get me reservations at the same place? John gave the okay." He tried his puppy dog look, if he actually had one.

"I know if anyone could get them for me on this short of notice, you would be the only one."

Looking exasperated, but lifting her chin up from her thin neck, she told Bailey she'd try, and when she told him an hour later that she had accomplished her mission, her posture showed her pride.

He picked his phone up and dialed a number he knew from memory.

"Dennis? This is Bailey, how are you doing? I wonder if I could come over and visit with you tonight? After dinner, say around 8:00 p.m? Yeah, thanks. If I bring a little libation, can you drink it?" Bailey smiled into the phone.

"Good, I'll see you around 8:00."

The day was still overcast and cold, with, of course, a strong wind blowing out of the northwest. The weather station had shown a storm front was being held in place by the jet stream. It was supposed to remain cold, cloudy and chances of small amounts of snow through the weekend.

This won't be bad. Winter is only lasting eight months now.

He called Dana and asked if she wanted to go to lunch and was pleasantly surprised by her acceptance. He told her he would pick her up at the library. He parked in front — screw that walking and freezing your ass off — and trotted upstairs and into the large entryway of the library. Dana was just finished reading a story to some young kids over in the children's section when she saw him, giving him a little wave. The kids looked over and some started giggling and pointing at him. When Dana finished reading, the kids left in a storm of laughing, squealing and shoving, all wanting to be the first out the door.

"Bye, Mrs. Calhoun, bye," they all shouted through the stampede.

Dana came up to Bailey, looking freshly scrubbed with a sparkle in her eyes.

"Bailey, you should see this. Someone sent a children's short story over the Internet. It's called 'The Magical Adventure.' The children just loved it. Would you like to see it?"

"Naw, that's all right, Dana, I find children's stories keep me awake wondering what's going to happen next." He smiled at her so his sarcasm wouldn't bite. Then, "Yeah, let me see it. Really."

She gave him the story, it was only three-quarters of a page long, and he quickly read it.

"I could use Mrs. Chandler to take me on a magical adventure; you aren't hinting you'd like a kid after all these years, are you?"

"No, Bailey. It's just nice to be around the innocence that kids have sometimes, rather than the 'been there, done that, don't wanna do this,' attitude we seem to have so often. Including you, Mr. Calhoun." The last she spoke with a smile so he knew he hadn't pissed her off.

"Well now, Mrs. Calhoun, that's because I have been there and done that. Though there's some things I still want to do, if you know what I mean."

She poked him in the ribs.

They went to lunch at Su Casa, a little Mexican food cafe in Sinclair, east of Rawlins a couple of miles. They went early because it got so busy, the lunch crowd would have to stand outside while waiting for a table. It was the best Mexican food Bailey had ever eaten. They got the last table, even being early, and ordered.

While they were waiting for their food, Bailey went over the facts, questions and conclusions again that he had come up with. He told her he was going to Denver the next day for a seminar and he was going to talk to Mike Hampston.

"I'm going over to Dennis's tonight to visit, would you like to come?"

"I would, Bailey, but I have to be at work almost every night this week and next. We have to do a manual inventory of all the books because we're converting over to a new computer system." Dana's face softened. "Ever since his wife died, I've thought we should do more for him. You've worked with him for five years, and now you're taking his position over so try to talk about something besides the job. He's probably feeling like he's being ousted from his life. I've heard once his retirement is official, he is going to move back to Las Vegas. Find out for me, will you?"

Their food arrived and they visited about the library while they ate.

When Bailey dropped her off, he looked at her with longing.

"Dana, I want you to move back in. If you will, either do it while I'm in Denver or wait until I'm back and I'll help you."

"I will, but since you're going to be gone and I have to work all this week, let's do it when you're back and I'm finished."

"All right, but don't tell Jenny what's going on, I want to surprise the cantankerous, sanctimonious —"

"Bailey, don't. Just don't. She's my friend, bitchy or not. And remember she works with abused women all the time, so her days aren't the most pleasant. You'd think the two of you would get along fine since you both have the same lousy attitude about the world."

"Christ, Dana. There goes the rest of my day. Now that's all I'll be thinking. Jenny and I sharing the same attitude. That'll make a guy want to vomit."

She slapped him on the back of his shoulder as he turned. "You just start being nicer to my friends," Dana said.

As he was walking out he felt better than he had in a long time. *Hell, maybe whoever sent that story to the library about Mrs. Chandler's magical adventure thought she'd take him.*

The wind had increased and he pulled his collar up around his neck when he got out of his truck in front of Dennis's house. He had a bottle of wine and was looking forward to the evening visit with his old friend. The porch light was on, giving off an inviting glow when Dennis opened the door.

"Bailey, come in, come in. Let me take your coat. Ah, you come bearing gifts." Taking Bailey's coat and the wine, he hung the jacket in the closet and took the wine to the kitchen.

"Let me open this and we'll let it breathe for a minute. Make yourself at home." The sound of the cork popping came from the kitchen.

Bailey had always liked Dennis's house. Oil paintings graced every wall. Some walls had six paintings hanging on them. He had once asked if they were originals; Dennis had laughed and said if they were the price was cheap. There were also several sculptures tastefully placed around the living room. The floor was hardwood and looked like oriental rugs were under the furniture. His living room couch, love seat and three chairs were all quality made and covered in a fine soft leather.

Bailey had once looked into buying a couch similar in style and the same brand but was dumbfounded by the price.

"Jesus Christ, do they have twenty-year mortgages for furniture?" He had asked Dana before she shushed him when the salesman approached.

That had been in Denver and he couldn't find an inexpensive one.

But Dennis made a nice salary and he lived well with it, something Bailey would like to have been able to do some day.

Dennis came in carrying two wine glasses half full and handed one to Bailey, then sat down in a comfortable looking recliner. "Sit, Bailey, and tell me to what do I owe the honor for the wine and visit?"

Bailey told him the story, starting with the Rock Springs incident and up to his present suspicions of Travis's discrepancy on the type of deaths and number of horses, as well as Williams's actions with the lease proposals and Calvin Knight. He told him how Frank heard some shots west of the old stage station and his flying out with Carl Toomes and finding the other twenty dead horses in the box canyon.

"I'm going to go to Denver tomorrow and I'll be there for a few days on business. I don't know if I should wait until I get some solid evidence or just talk to Williams now and see if he'll listen without telling me it's not my job anymore." Bailey took a small sip of the wine. *Damn, that tasted good.* "Right now, all the evidence is circumstantial." He told Dennis he even felt stupid thinking that a conspiracy might be going on.

Dennis sat back after Bailey finished, with his eyes half closed, his head tilted forward as if he was praying.

"Bailey, if I were you, I would talk to John tomorrow before you leave. I find it hard to fathom him being involved in anything like what you have described. I think you will find that John has a very valid answer for the actions that are bothering you. So, talk to him first."

Bailey had been sitting on the edge of his chair while Dennis was talking. He visibly relaxed when Dennis had assured Bailey he didn't think there was anything sinister going on.

"All right, Dennis. I'll do it. Now, how are you feeling after your surgery?"

"It's amazing, Bailey. They lay you on the table, and then split your sternum from top to bottom using what look like sheep shears, and then pull your ribs out of the way. I've got a video of the surgery, would you like to see it?"

"No thanks, my stomach doesn't have the strength to see something like a man being field dressed. So are you healed completely now?"

"I still can't lift anything heavy. My sternum is wired together and they say if I was to strain too much by picking up something heavy, or receive a blow to my chest, it could kill me. So I'm just taking it easy. I've made some good investments in the stock market so I don't have to worry about money. Of course, I still get my salary until I'm officially retired." He stood up and offered Bailey some more wine.

"One more quick glass, then I've got to be going. I'm going to talk to John like you suggested before I leave tomorrow. You've really helped me, thanks, Dennis." The wine was down with three swallows. He went over to the closet and slipped his coat from the hanger. Putting it on, he opened the door and paused.

"I'm not going to tell John I talked to you. By the way, you're both from Las Vegas, what was he like there?"

Dennis smiled as he thought back. "Believe it or not, he was a bit of a hell raiser. We weren't in the same division; I was upstairs in the lease department and he was a regional assistant supervisor. But I saw him several times in the casinos gambling. From what the rumors were, he was quite the drinker and gambler. That's why he transferred here. Supposedly it was a take it or quit, you're embarrassing us proposition, but I then heard he had gone to a psychiatrist and he was helped immeasurably." He held the door for Bailey and was starting to look a little fatigued.

"You need to take it easy and get some rest." Bailey shook Dennis's hand and held it. "I want you to enjoy your retirement and not worry about this. Life's too damn short."

"Not to worry, my friend. I intend to learn how to fly fish and how to tie my own flies." Dennis smiled warmly at Bailey.

"Dennis, thanks again for the advice and rumors; I'll keep my mouth shut." He went to his truck and got in then sat for a moment before starting the engine. *Who would ever think that John Williams was a boozer and a gambler. Wonders never cease.*

The porch light went out as Bailey drove away from the house. I'll bet

Dennis doesn't fly fish very many times, Bailey thought, watching the dark house recede in the rearview mirror. You don't spend thirty years in a job then just forget about it.

He drove past Jenny's and saw a light on. Wondering if it was Dana, he almost stopped but decided against it. He was going to have a busy day tomorrow.

The taste of the wine still lingered in his mouth and mind. There was still a six pack of beer in the fridge; *one* couldn't hurt anything, could it?

Early the next morning, the feeling of fucking up royally sat heavy with him when the six empty beer cans came into his sight. With the heavy burden of realization, Bailey wearily got out of bed with the thought of climbing back on the wagon. *God, I sound like an alky.*

*   *   *   *   *   *   *   *   *

Williams opened the office door and saw Bailey waiting for him. Unlocking the door to his office, Williams said, "I thought you were going to Denver today, Bailey?"

"I am, but I'd like to talk to you first, John. I need to go over some things and get some straight answers."

He watched Williams stiffen, then get some coffee and invite Bailey into his office, motioning him to sit in a chair.

"Go ahead, ask your questions, though I don't know what you mean by straight answers."

"Okay. Let me tell you what I see going on and you set me straight." Bailey said.

Williams nodded his head.

"Travis said he found twelve horses on the refuge that were dead from winterkill. There were fifteen and they had all been shot. I was looking over some lease proposals and found one from Golden Eagle wanting a lease to start gas exploration beginning in July on the horse refuge. The proposal is missing from my desk and Dora told me she saw you take some papers from it. I was also told that you've been having quite a few conferences with Calvin Knight. So, John, you tell me."

99

Williams's face turned beet red and he sat straight in his chair.

"First of all, I resent you investigating me and the people in this office. The explanation is very simple regarding my dealings with Calvin. He contacted me the other day and asked if I could check on a lease proposal he had made some time ago. You had left the office and were gone most of the morning, so I found it on your desk and called him. He had thought, mistakenly, he could submit a lease proposal on the area he had previously leased and lost due to the fact it had been made into the refuge. He thought by having leased it before, he would be granted grandfather rights." Williams sipped his coffee, then continued.

"In this case the area was the southern quadrant of the refuge. When I told him that he couldn't get it, he wanted his lease request to stand in perpetual submission. So, in other words, his past lease and request for a lease would always be attached to the area's scope of usage." Williams looked Bailey in the eye.

"Now, concerning Travis, we will just have to ask him when he's back about the discrepancy in his report on the cause of death of the horses. Are your questions answered satisfactorily?" He almost sneered after the last sentence.

"Yeah, all except the amount of time you're spending with Knight. It wouldn't take several days to explain this to him."

Williams's eyes sparkled. "It's really none of your business, Calhoun, but I'm going to tell you. Mr. Knight has offered me a job with his gas exploration company. He wants me to do some lobbying for him in Washington. We're negotiating. If I am offered and accept the job, then you can do whatever you want about advancing. Now don't you think you should be leaving for Denver?"

Bailey stared at him for a few moments trying to decide if Williams was playing him for a dumb shit or if he was telling the truth. Deciding he would hold his judgment until he talked to Travis and Rudy Maes, he rose to leave.

"Keep this in mind, John. Somebody killed those horses and I'm going to find out who. And when I do, God help them."

Without a backward glance, he walked down to his desk. Dana was at work when he called and told her he would see her Friday or Saturday, Bailey went to his truck and left for Denver.

Chapter Thirteen

When he hit Northglenn on I-25 south, the downtown buildings were barely visible through the smog. All four lanes were jammed with cars and it seemed like every one of them wanted to run his ass off the road.

Thinking he'd like to take a little detour, he turned west on 104th Avenue and stopped at Gunther Tooties to eat lunch. He'd seen a lot of commercials about the diner on TV and the burgers and beer looked good. He finished his hamburger by chasing it down with what was left of a cold chocolate shake. It was so busy he'd had to eat at the counter, but he didn't mind. It was in the style of the old diners from year's back and he enjoyed his meal.

When he got back onto the freeway, the traffic had dropped off to only three lanes being jam-packed and trying to run over his ass. He got into the slow lane until he was able to take the downtown exit, then found the Comfort Suites and left his truck with the valet parking. He really didn't want to drive around downtown Denver, too many cars, and not enough streets. *If I got lost I'd be here forever, like the guy on the MTA.*

After checking in at the front desk he took an elevator to the fourteenth floor where his room overlooked Stout Street. He was just across the street from the Brown Palace so he could walk to the seminar. He turned the TV on and laid down on the bed, not realizing how tired he was until his head started drooping when he tried reading a pamphlet. Deciding the hell with it, he got up and went to the bar on the ground floor. *I'm not drinking any fucking booze.* There were several men and a few women he saw that he knew worked for the BLM and he had met over the years at conferences. Richard Tyler was one he knew and Bailey saw him standing at the bar talking to a large-breasted woman. Her hair color was from a bottle, her boobs were pumped up about three sizes more than what they should have been and if she took her sweater off, Bailey would have bet $100 that the word hooker would have been written on her back.

Richard was a party man and it looked like he'd already had too many drinks. She was the black widow spider closing in on the fly. Easing between Tyler and a man talking on his cell phone, Bailey reached over and slid Tyler's money away from the gal and next to Tyler's hands. Tyler looked over in a drunken haze.

"Whatta you think you're doing? Calhoun! How're you hanging?"

"I didn't know you were bringing your wife, Richard. Usually you're by yourself at these things."

"Shit, this isn't my wife. This is Molly; she was here when I came in. Asked me if I wanted a good time. I think I'm too screwed up now, because the only good time would be trying to find it in my pants."

With that, he laughed out loud and said to Molly, "I think we're too late, kiddo, better find someone else."

Molly gave Bailey the finger, picked up her drink and sat down at a table with three guys telling jokes.

"Christ, that was close. Sometimes I think my brain is below my buckle. I get a little carried away at these things." Tyler said. "So, what's happening, Bailey? They shook hands and Bailey pointed his finger for the bartender to bring a beer for Tyler.

"Club soda for me," he told the bartender as the beer was delivered to Richard.

"I see you're on the wagon, I oughta be. How have you been doing?"

"I've been busy. Our assistant supervisor is retiring and I'm getting stuck in his place. The money and grade are better, but I don't want to be stuck in an office all the time. How about you?" He lifted up his glass of club soda that had just been delivered and gave a mock salute, then took a swallow.

"Same old shit. People bitching about the ranchers controlling access to the land, ranchers bitching about people tearing up their roads and fences and shit." Tyler started waving at the smoke hanging in the air away from his face.

"Let's grab a table, these smoke stacks are gonna choke me out." Picking up his beer Tyler maneuvered around some tables and sat at an empty one across the room from Molly.

"I like this lounge, it's classy." Bailey said. The walls were dark wood and the bar shined with a glossy reflection. "I like the carpet and music. Doesn't run a guy out." The music coming from hidden speakers was quiet background music. It hung on the edge, not loud, but not so low that you would strain to hear it. Sitting down next to Tyler, Bailey took a sip of the club soda.

"Didn't you work with John Williams, Richard? Over in Vegas or somewhere around that part of the country?"

"Yeah, I worked with him in Montana before he transferred. He was the top dog at the regional office in Bozeman when I was there. You work for him in Rawlins now, don't you?"

Bailey said he did and asked what Tyler thought of Williams.

"Well, he acted like he had a broom stuck up his ass most of the time. He catered to the important, moneyed people. What really pissed most of us off was he wouldn't socialize with anybody unless they were a manager or a big shot. You know, something like that."

"Just between you and me, did you ever think he was dirty?" Bailey didn't like putting it that way; rumors could start and ruin a man if they spread, but he needed to know what kind of person Williams was, or at least perceived by his former co-workers.

"I don't know, Bailey. He wouldn't steal the petty cash, but I always thought he wanted to be someone with money and influence. If he could make his way up the rung — ah, I'm not sure what he'd do, Bailey."

"Hey, enough of this shit, I'll flip to see who buys dinner." Bailey thought he had gleaned a little useful information and didn't want to push Tyler anymore. Losing the flip, they went to the dining room and ate the hotel's buffet. When they finished eating, Bailey told Tyler he was going to hit the rack early because he had some things to do before the seminar.

"Come on, Bailey, let's hit a couple of places first, then you can act like an old lady. Hell, the thing doesn't start until after lunch."

"All right, I'm not staying out and getting drunk with your ass, though. I've only got tomorrow morning to get some business done."

"Isn't that typical of the government," Tyler said. "They schedule this in the afternoon the first day so people won't have to stay a night to make an early start time, then they go for nine hours and finish in the afternoon the next day and you have to stay overnight anyway."

"You know why, don't you?" Bailey replied. "This way your weekend is ruined because you either get back late or you stay overnight again because you won't get home in one shot. Then they can piss and moan that you spent too much money on lodging and food."

"How did you make it down here on the day before? You only gotta drive, what, a couple hundred miles?" Tyler asked.

Signing the bill and putting both dinners on his room tab, Bailey said, "Believe it or not, Williams thought I should come down and stay an extra day to get a break. Maybe the broom broke off."

They left the hotel and walked to several hotel bars in the downtown area. Around midnight they returned and after saying the usual, "Let's keep in touch. Right, sometime we'll get together and do some fishing." Knowing they never would, they went to their rooms.

Getting up several times to use the bathroom, Bailey knew it was from drinking all the club soda he had that night while he was with Tyler. He couldn't sleep worth a shit. The next morning after showering and dressing, Bailey called Rudy Maes's cell number and got his voice mail. "Rudy, this is Bailey, I was calling to see if you got any results yet on the bullets? I'm in Denver now and will be home Friday night late. If you have anything, call me at my home number and leave a message if I'm not there."

He hung the phone up then decided to walk over to the Federal Building on 19th and Stout. If Hampston wasn't busy he might be able to show Bailey around. The FBI was located several floors below and he had never seen or been in it.

United States Treasury, Secret Service Division, was the first thing Bailey saw as the elevator doors opened. He gave his name at the reception counter and asked to speak to Agent Hampston. The girl pushed a button on the telephone, speaking into it softly. She asked Bailey to wait in the reception area. Agent Hampston would be out shortly. In the old days, teletypes would be chattering and phones ringing with echoes of footsteps on the linoleum floor. Now there was near silence, computers transmitting and receiving information, the sound of people walking being dampened by the carpet and the phones chiming instead of ringing.

"Hey, Bailey, long time no see." Walking up with his hand out Hampston shook Bailey's hand then escorted him to his office. Hampston had blond, receding hair, was about six feet tall and looked to be in fair shape. His suit was form fitting and didn't seem to be hiding a gut. Bailey pulled his stomach in; he and Mike were the same age. Handing Bailey a cup of coffee, Mike leaned back in his chair, blowing over his coffee. "What's been going on in the life of the infamous BLM Investigator?" he asked.

"I'll be lucky if infamous doesn't turn into fired." Bailey told Mike the story from the beginning and up through confronting Williams the day before.

"Can you check something for me? It's not official and I don't know if you could do it on the side, but I'd like a background check on Williams and a man by the name of Calvin Knight." Bailey set a piece of paper on Hampston's desk. "Here's Williams's DOB and social security number, but I couldn't get Knight's. He owns the Golden Eagle Gas and Exploration Company. He's in his early 60's and I think he came up from Texas back in the 1960's. Sorry I don't have the numbers but when you're an infamous BLM investigator, it's tough to get them from anyone."

Hampston wrote the information down on a pad, gave Bailey a once-over look, then tore the page off and stuck it in a desk drawer. "Asking for this stuff on your boss is pretty risky, Bailey. Do you know what you might be getting into, especially if he finds out?"

"Yeah, I do, I'll take the chance. There's been talk he sticks his nose up the asses of big business people and had a drinking and gambling problem in Vegas. Don't worry, this isn't going to be public knowledge. Just mine, so I have a handle on him. As they say, 'A conspirator or not a conspirator, that is the question.' If you don't want to do it, Mike, I understand completely, no problemo."

"Let me look into it, Bailey. I'll see if I can round up this Knight's social number and DOB. Do a little nosing around with Vegas. It will have to be when I can work it in, though, 'cause we've got some counterfeiting going on that's taking a lot of my time." He stood up and smiled. "But now, let's go eat. I've been saving myself for lunch at Duffy's when you said you'd buy."

They walked down to 16th and Court Place and were seated as soon as they entered. Bailey hadn't been there in years, but he liked the Irish theme, dark hard wooden floors and the permeating smell of corned beef and cabbage.

Giving their order to the waiter, Bailey hunched over the table. "The thing on this case, Mike, is I'm not sure of the time sequence. This old guy that lives out around there told me it happened within a couple of days of each other. How and if that relates to the Red Desert thing, I won't know until I get the ballistics back from the S.O. in Rock Springs." Bailey lifted the water glass to his lips and drained half in two swallows.

"It sounds like that might have been before the refuge killings. What really stumps me is why someone would kill that many horses in one place like the canyon. I didn't see any single horses dead when I flew it last weekend. That makes me believe that it's not some ass-hole driving around and taking pot shots at a horse or two. The ones in the Red Desert were killed in a canyon, so it's mass killings for some disgusting, crazy reason." He felt the frustration when he finished talking.

"Let's knock off the work talk and enjoy the food. If you have time after we eat I'd like you to take me through the FBI office, if you can." Bailey asked.

They exited the elevator on the eighteenth floor. "Notice that the Bureau is two floors below us?" Hampston opened the big glass doors of the FBI office. "I believe that indicates the top dog. They're on the eighteenth and we're on the twentieth. The higher up, the mightier."

"Isn't the District BLM office in this building?" Bailey knew it wasn't.

"Yes, yes it is, Mr. Calhoun. You'll have to take the elevator to the second sub-basement, first door past the lady's toilets." Hampston's laugh came out as a high-pitched squeal which surprised most people who didn't know him, since he was a big man.

Mike introduced Bailey to Agent Joseph Flemming, typical fed. Tall, young, good shape, short hair and a nice suit. Hampston left, telling Bailey he had to get back to work and they would talk later. Agent Flemming gave Bailey the tour usually reserved for police officers. When they were finished, Bailey thanked him and walked back to his hotel. He gathered his notebook and ran over to the Brown Palace, finding the conference room just as the introductions were being made. The afternoon session ended with Bailey wondering what the hell everyone had talked about; he had been in a state of total oblivion during the seminar.

Tyler looked him up and they decided to go out on the town with some people from the group Tyler had shared a table with. They walked along Larimer Street going down to Larimer Square, which Bailey hadn't been around since it had changed from being part of the Bowery to an upscale area with some fine restaurants and shops. They went to several microbreweries, ate crab legs at the Ratskeller on the government, and eventually made their way back to the hotel through a myriad of bars.

Bailey flopped down on his bed, surprised that he hadn't had any beer the entire night. He thought it would be interesting to see how the other guys would fare in the morning. The blinking message light on his phone got his attention.

"I have a message light on," he said to the operator.

"Yes sir, a Deputy Maes wanted you to call him at his home when you returned to your room. Here's the number if you have a pen ready."

Dialing the number he felt some anxiety start to build.

"Rudy, Bailey. Hope this isn't too late to call. What's going on?"

"Bailey, the bullets match! So far we have three different guns being used. We know now the bastards that killed our horses killed yours also. Unfortunately, we still don't have a fucking clue to who the shooters are. Hell, we don't even know if there was more than one." He sounded like he'd drunk some beers before Bailey had called him.

"How'd you know where I was staying, Rudy?"

"I called your office and your secretary, Dora, gave me the hotel's name. Don't worry, I didn't tell her about the bullets, just said I needed to talk to you. Damn, I hope this is a break. It's going be up to you to make something out of this. We're at a dead end here unless the anonymous caller squeals."

"Okay, Rudy. Thanks for getting the info so fast. I'll keep in touch."

He ran his fingers through his hair then added the latest information to his notebook. He wanted the seminar to be over early so he could get back home. Things seemed to be picking up speed.

Chapter Fourteen

His private line was ringing. Reaching over to his telephone he lifted the handset. "Just a minute." He said. Walking over to his office door he told his secretary to hold his calls then closed the door and went back to his desk.

Picking up the phone again, he said, "I hope you aren't calling about another problem." Calvin Knight's usual demeanor was starting to fade. Usually, he was robust and outgoing. Lately he seemed to be withdrawing into himself, a little more each day. He was a man seemingly under great pressure.

"Calvin," the voice on the phone said. "We seem to have a small problem." Knight's eyes rolled up and he let out a big sigh. "Bailey Calhoun found the other horses in the canyon and knows something's up. I thought you were going to get a backhoe out there and bury them?"

"I was. Streck took it out with a trailer and got the damn thing stuck. By the time they were out of the mess the sun was coming up and they were worried someone might come out or see them. That Streck's crazy. Somehow he knows about Calhoun and I think he's made it into a contest. Him

111

against Calhoun." Opening his desk drawer he pulled out a glass and a bottle of Black Velvet, then poured himself a small amount and knocked it down in one gulp.

"Calvin, I hear you drinking. Go easy, we're fine."

"It's easy for you to say that. You're not the one that has those blood-thirsty scavengers after your business."

"Calvin, Calvin. It was your foolishness on the gambling tables that put you so much in debt to these people. Calhoun is suspicious about the lease proposal and he thinks Travis is involved with the dead horses."

"Well, shit! What're we going to do? If things aren't done and in place by the 15th of June, my business is gone. I won't have anything." His voice cracked with desperation.

"I believe," the voice spoke in gentle tones, "we should give Calhoun a message. I think having Streck pay Calhoun's wife a little visit, and, if you'll pardon the expression, 'Fuck her up', he can leave a message for Calhoun to drop what he's doing. I should think he would, it's not that big of a deal, really."

"Or," Knight poured himself another shot, "Bailey will go ballistic and might screw everyone up. I know him. I've known him for thirty years and I remember some of the things he did when he went ape shit. If we hurt his wife and he finds out we were involved, I honestly think he'll kill us."

"If this doesn't work, Calvin, we might have to look at doing away with Calhoun."

"Jesus Christ! How can you say that so calmly? I don't know if I want to go that far."

"You let me know, Calvin. If you don't, you won't have anything. And remember, the people you owe money to won't write it off as a tax deduction. As you can imagine, they don't pay taxes on these kinds of things. It's up to you, so decide, and let me know."

There was a "click", then silence as Calvin held the phone to his ear. He was sweating though the office was cool. He placed the receiver down and thought, *am I ready to give all this up and maybe die, because of some damn wild horses? Bailey shouldn't have been so nosy. He should have believed Travis about the winterkill.* Having found resolution he felt as if a weight were lifted off his shoulders. He had heard when someone is going to commit suicide, they'll sometimes act happy and relieved. They've resolved their problem. Calvin Knight resolved his problem, except it wasn't suicide.

Calvin left work and drove to his house. His thoughts were in the past, how he had first come to town back in '64, and made a small fortune. He had gained prominence in the community, and was often asked for his opinion and spoke at various functions. He loved all of it. He was in every organization that a prominent citizen should be.

He turned at Sheep Hill, a street of homes built in the early 1900's for the big sheep ranchers. Most were gone now, either dead or moved away and retired, selling their ranches to big corporations that paid them the big dollars. He had bought his house, a large, three-story home with terraces and a huge front porch, from old Doc Clinton when he retired back in '80. Calvin immediately put $20,000 into remodeling and it was the showplace of the town. It still was, but not for long, as Calvin didn't have the extra money to keep putting into it. A beautiful home but the damn thing took lot of money to maintain, let alone continual redecoration.

"Margo, I'm home." Calvin bellowed out as he came in from the garage. Not seeing her in the kitchen or living room he went upstairs. Lying on her back, a slight snoring coming from her lips, his wife, Margo, slept in a drunken stupor. Apparently she had enjoyed herself in her social circle that day. She volunteered at the hospital, ran charities and drank a fifth of Lord Calvert with her friends daily. When there was a rare day her friends weren't around, she was able to drink most of the bottle by herself. She was oblivious to Calvin's financial situation, insisting they keep up with their peers in the social race.

Calvin looked on his wife of nearly 40 years. Eyes hollow, slack-jawed and her face lined with wrinkles, she appeared to be fifteen years older than she was. Sometimes Calvin and Margo didn't talk or see each other for a week. They had separate bedrooms and neither seemed to mind the current arrangement.

He went downstairs to his den and poured himself a drink. Sitting in his chair behind his desk he thought of all the things that had to be done for everything to work. *Is it worth it?* He asked himself. His eyes took in the den with the oak desk which had been handmade in the Amana Colonies in Iowa, the silk draperies, the magnificent home and being important and recognized. *Yes...yes, it is worth it.*

Chapter Fifteen

The phone rang twice before he picked it up. "Yeah..."

"We think a message to Calhoun would be appropriate. One that will make him think about forgetting his inquiries into the horse situation. Possibly an accident involving his wife or if you prefer, something happening to Calhoun himself. It's entirely up to you."

A smile spread on his face; Streck answered with one word.

"Good." He hung the phone up. Grabbing a jacket and leaving his room, he got into his car and drove down Spruce to the Sunset Motel. Lynch opened the curtain on the window and saw Streck approaching. He opened the door and immediately started whining.

"Christ, Streck, how much longer do we have to stay in this joint?"

"This is your lucky night, Lynch. You and Gomez take the Pontiac and go back to Denver. I'll keep the truck. Check in at the Idle Hours Bar on East Colfax. If I don't get a hold of you, come back Wednesday." He opened his coat pocket and took out a roll of fifty-dollar bills. Counting out forty, he gave Lynch and Gomez each twenty of the bills.

"Hey, what's this bullshit? We're suppose to get $2000 a piece." Lynch had turned red and his voice rose in volume. "Fuck this! I want all my money."

He was thrown to the floor with a hand around his throat — thumb and fingers pinching his windpipe closed. "When we're done, asshole. You don't come back when I need you, it puts me in a bind." He relaxed his fingers and stood up, facing Gomez.

"What about you, Gomez, you got a problem with this?"

His grin showed all of his white teeth. Shaking his head no, he swung his left fist at Streck's jaw. Pushing the punch off with his right hand, Streck caught Gomez flush in the mouth. Blood flew and pieces of teeth dropped along with Gomez to the carpet. He held his hands to his mouth.

"You futter. You boke my teefh." He moaned and rolled onto his knees.

Streck went into the bathroom and ran some water on a towel. Throwing it at Gomez he said, "Don't get any blood on the carpet. Now...you two got a problem with this?"

Both Lynch and Gomez were still on the floor. Lynch slowly rose and sat on the bed. "You didn't have to do that. We was pissed about the money. We weren't gonna fuck with you."

Streck tossed the keys to the car on the top of the dresser. "Gimme the keys to the truck." He caught them in the air as Lynch pulled them out of his pocket and threw them to Streck. Closing the door on his way out, Streck said, "Trust me, I'm not going to fuck you over either."

He started the truck and drove west to the Interstate, made a half circle and ended up going east toward Laramie.

He drove 70 mph, swinging around the refinery town of Sinclair, through Arlington, then into Laramie.

He found the local Super Walmart on the east end of town. He had about forty minutes before it closed. Picking out ten spray cans of misty green metal paint, a thought came to him and he went over to the sporting goods side and bought a hunting knife with an eight-inch blade and scabbard.

"That will be $62.38; will this be cash or charge?" The cashier had a pleasant expression on her face but acted itchy. Streck figured she was anxious for the store to close.

Not saying anything he gave her a fifty, ten and a five. Giving him his change, she smiled and said, "Thank you for shopping at Walmart, please come again." The checker shut the light off, showing her station was closed.

Streck drove to Arby's and picked up a half-dozen sandwiches, then stopped at a drive-in liquor store and bought a six pack of Bud. No use trying to buy Old Sheridan in this podunk place.

He left Laramie on Highway 30, the old, two-lane road to Rawlins. Around 11:15 p.m. he stopped at the New Moon Motel in Rock River and rented a room. Inside, he lay on the bed eating the sandwiches and chasing them down with the Bud. The town was so small there wasn't cable or satellite, just antenna. All he could pick up was KNCN out of Denver and the single TV station out of Cheyenne.

There was a news summary on KNCN. The picture was three years old and didn't look a lot like him.

"A suspect in the murder of Patsy Mae Brinkman has been identified as Orville James Streck, a white male, six feet one inch tall, weighing 230 lbs. He has short, black hair and a large tattoo on the right side of his neck. The victim and Streck were seen together the night of the murder. Streck was recently paroled from the Colorado State Penitentiary and is considered extremely dangerous. He was last seen driving a 1978 cream colored Buick LeSabre, Colorado license, AAC-30771. If seen, do not try to apprehend. Call your local police department or dial 911. As you might remember, Ms. Brinkman's body was discovered two weeks ago, sexually assaulted and dead in a field west of 6th Avenue and C-470."

"Shit!" He flung his beer can into the wall then slammed the TV off.

*   *   *   *   *   *   *   *   *

"Oh, Jesus Christ!" Calvin Knight thought he was going to throw up. Staring at the TV he couldn't believe what he had just heard. "God, this is all I need. Streck, wanted for murder and his picture on TV."

He dialed the number and poured a big glass of whiskey, taking a long swallow just as the phone was answered.

"What the hell are we going to do? Did you see the news?" He was breathing hard, almost screaming and the thought of a heart attack entered his mind. *I'm going to have a heart attack and die. Jesus Christ, help.*

"Calvin, Calvin, slow down, take it easy. We're almost finished with Mr. Streck. When we don't need him anymore, I'll make a call and we'll never see him again. Now, take some deep breaths. Lord, you're going to give yourself a heart attack, and that certainly won't do me any good." The man talked some more and Calvin's heart rate decreased.

Another sip of whiskey and Calvin thought, sure, he won't be found here. *No one can tie me in with him.* He hung the telephone up and for the one-hundredth time, wondered what he had gotten himself into.

    *   *   *   *   *   *   *   *

The picture had shown him clean-shaved. His beard had been growing for three weeks and was thick. It looked as if he had grown it some time ago. The tattoo was a problem. Seeing his reflection in the mirror he tried hiding it several different ways. Finally, he put his neckerchief around his neck and tied it like the cowboys used to, before they pulled it over their noses to rob a bank. *This ain't bad.* He thought it covered the tattoo enough so it wasn't obvious.

Leaving the motel, he drove around the town until he found an abandoned barn at the end of a dirt road. Deciding the odds were against the town having a full-time cop, he parked inside the barn and took the cans of spray paint out of the truck. He got the knife and slid it down into his boot thinking, *I'll go out in style.*

The only thing heard for twenty minutes was the shaking and hissing of the spray cans. When he was done, the white and brown was covered in a medium green. He felt confident that the truck wouldn't be connected with anything he'd used it for.

The knife felt good in his boot and he wondered if it would be Calhoun or his old lady he'd use it on. Probably both.

118

When he left Rock River three hours later, after the paint had dried, he decided to beat up the woman first. Figuring if Calhoun was any kind of a man, he'd want to take Streck on, mano-a-mano. Knight had told him about Calhoun. A cop for a while, he was a big ex-marine, tough. He had seen Calhoun through the binoculars talking to the fucking old bum a week after they had killed the horses. Streck had been out there to find and shoot some more, but had seen the truck and the jeep down by the sand dune.

Streck smiled as he thought about his encounter with Frank. The nice, sharp crack his neck made when one hand pushed on a shoulder and the other pulled on the old man's chin.

Streck had driven up to the shanty cabin and parked next to the old red jeep. The front door opened and Frank stuck his head out. "What'd ya need? I ain't got no business with you."

"I want to talk to you. Just take a minute." Streck climbed the steps and laid a shoulder on the door. He saw Frank cringe a little, then the door opened all the way.

"You can come in, but I'm leaving here in a few minutes. Want do ya want?"

"Who were you talking to the other day? At the sand dunes."

"When?" Frank shuffled back toward the wall.

"You know when." Streck grabbed the front of Frank's shirt and cuffed him twice across the face.

"Don't hit me no more." He whimpered. "Calhoun stopped and asked me if I knowed anything about the horses you killed. I didn't tell him nothing. I swear!" He flinched when Streck doubled a fist and held it in front of Frank's face.

"You're lying to me, old man." The fist struck Frank above his left eye. Another fist buried itself in his kidney. Streck hammered him to the ground then picked him up.

"What'd you tell him, Frank?" A finger and thumb pinching the old man's nose brought tears from the sharp pain.

119

And Frank told him everything. He even made up a couple things so Streck wouldn't hit him again.

"That's all, everything we talked about." Frank put his hand up in a stopping motion. "Why don't you let me go now? I ain't sayin' nothing to nobody again."

"You're right, you ain't saying nothing." Streck spun Frank around grabbing his chin and yanking with one hand and shoving against Frank's shoulder with the other hand. Old brittle bones snap fairly easy. Frank was dead when he hit the floor.

Medicine Bow was another small town that died when the interstate was built. Streck took his time getting to Rawlins by driving around Hanna, a coal-mining town, then getting on I-80 at Walcott Junction. It was four in the afternoon when he stopped at a small café on the west end of Rawlins. After eating, he went back to his room and dialed a number.

When it was answered he asked a question, "Where do I find Calhoun's old lady? The library...what's she look like? Doesn't sound too bad. What's she drive? TV news? Yeah, I saw it. I didn't kill her; I was as surprised as you were. No sweat, nothing I can't handle."

The room was paid for until the end of the week, so he wouldn't have to be around too many people where he might stick out. He didn't think the young desk clerk who had checked him in would remember the tattoo. *I covered it with my neckerchief.*

Streck thought of a plan for Calhoun's wife. Maybe screw her up just enough so it won't take long for her to be back out on the street, then really fuck her up. He cracked his knuckles as he savored the thought of hurting the woman twice.

He looked the telephone number up in the phone book and dialed it. When it was answered he asked, "Could you tell me how long the library stays open on Saturday?"

"Yes sir, we close at 7:00 p.m. Is there anything I can help you with?" The voice was that of a pleasant-sounding woman.

"No thanks." He wondered if that was Calhoun's wife. Wouldn't it be ironic to have her tell him when she would be available to have the shit beat out of her? He hung the phone up and with a smile building on his face, thought, *Yes sir, things is looking up.*

*   *   *   *   *   *   *   *   *

Bailey rode into town with an east wind, getting to his house about ten p.m. He saw the neighbors had fed Callie like he'd asked. He let her in with him since he'd been gone for three days.

There was a message on his answering machine. Pushing the play button, he got a beer out of the fridge while he listened.

"Bailey, I've been working late these last two nights, but I'll get off Saturday night at seven. I'll close a little early and thought maybe we could go out for dinner. My treat. Call me tomorrow before noon. Love ya."

Things were getting better. Bailey laughed thinking how she would react to the arrowhead necklace he had bought her in Denver. *She'll probably think I ripped them off from out north.*

He poured the beer down the drain and went to bed. Looking out the window at the clouds moving in, he thought about his night coming up with Dana.

When Bailey woke up the next morning the sun was streaming in the window. Surprisingly, it was calm out. A true spring day. He looked over and found Callie sleeping next to him, on Dana's side.

"What're you doing, Callie? She lifted her head up, wagged her tail then flopped it back down on the pillow, closing her eyes tight. He had forgotten to put her out for the night and she had slipped onto the bed. Bailey gently prodded her off, where she gave him a disdainful look and went into the kitchen.

He was in a good mood and he knew why. It was because he and Dana were feeling like they used to. Enjoying each other's company. Knowing there wasn't any way he could, he still wanted to try to give himself a break from the dead horses. He was going to try and putter around the house until he called Dana. For some reason, he felt like he was courting her rather than being married to her. Maybe she should leave every three or four months to recharge their romance. Bailey grinned and thought he might have to mention it to her someday.

121

The sound of the power rake was loud and obnoxious when he started raking the back yard. Callie chased after him barking and trying to catch the wheels. Bailey finally put her in her kennel until he finished with both the front and back. By then it was after eleven and he hurriedly put the lawn machinery back into the shed, then went into the house and called Dana at the library.

"Dana, what are the plans for tonight?" He could hear books being moved in the background.

"Well, I thought I'd come out to the house around seven thirty, and then take my man out to eat at the Steak House. Fill him with steak and a beer or two then get him home and ravage him. What do you think?"

"Maybe we should go out at noon." If he had grinned any wider, his face would have split in two. "That's great, Dana, are you going to come back and stay, permanent?"

"Yes I am, Bailey. I've missed you. We can pick up my clothes Sunday from Jenny's. I haven't told her yet, just that I was going out to dinner with someone. I've also found out something I believe will put you in my debt forever. I researched the Wild Horse Refuge Bill and found some interesting items I think will surprise you."

"Tell me now, you've already got my interest."

"No...No———tonight. The waiting makes it all the better. I've got to go now, Bailey, so I'll be at the house around seven thirty. Love you."

Bailey looked at the phone after she had hung up and gently replaced the receiver. *What the hell did she find out?* With eight hours to kill he decided to clean the house up and have it ready for her.

Around two in the afternoon, sweat dripping off his forehead he wondered how housewives could do this shit day in and day out. *Christ, it was hard work.* He shut the vacuum cleaner off and picked up the telephone. As he waited for the phone to be answered he put some dirty dishes in the dishwasher.

"Cars are Us, how may I direct your call?" A perky sounding operator asked.

"I would like to speak to the esteemed, James McConroy."

"May I say who's calling, please?"

"Tell him this is Robert Trenton with the IRS, and we're waiting for his tax money."

"One moment, please." He could hear the clicks as the line was transferred to another phone.

"This is Jim McConroy, who's calling?" He could feel the steam in the line, he figured Jim knew he was being screwed with; he just wasn't sure who was doing it.

McConroy was Bailey's best friend even though he didn't live in Rawlins. A tough street fighter from years back, they'd served together in Vietnam and McConroy had been medvac'd out with Bailey. During their prime, they were two of the tougher men in town. He had moved to California after marrying a cute little blonde named Linda, several years younger than him.

"This is your worst nightmare, ass-hole."

"Bailey, you bastard. I hear Dana found herself a young stud so you're not getting any pussy now." He was always quick to be a smart-ass.

"He's not a bad stud. I mean, he's funny and interesting, hung like a horse but he's fun to be around. I like him. Dana's happy so I'm happy. But enough of me. I heard from the rumor mill that Linda found herself a new girl friend. Says anything is better than having a fat bastard like you on top of her, grunting like a pig for thirty seconds. Your endurance has improved by the way."

Jim was laughing over the phone so hard that Bailey got laughing. Two minutes later, wiping tears off his face he said, "I just thought I'd call. Things between Dana and I have been a little rocky but it's looking good now."

"The last time we talked it sounded kind of shitty," Jim said. "I'm glad things are going good. What's new with the job?"

With the opening, Bailey told him about the killing of the horses and what he had been doing about it.

"Sounds screwed up. Maybe I ought to come back and pull your dumb ass out of the fire."

"I'd take you up on it, Jim, but you'd probably get lost in the airport and take up with the cleaning man. How would I ever explain that to Linda?"

They visited for another ten minutes and with Jim promising that he and Linda would come to visit soon and Bailey promising he and Dana would be coming to California, they hung up.

Ahh, that crazy bastard, wish he would move here.

He chugged a diet coke and went down the hallway with the vacuum, furniture polish and scrub brushes.

Chapter Sixteen

Her car was parked in the lot at the back of the library. All the other cars had left except for hers and there was only one room in the library with its lights still on. Streck backed in at the corner of the lot so he could reach her in seconds.

Dusk passed and the night grew darker. The remaining light went out. A couple of minutes later he saw her locking the side door of the building and walking toward the parking lot, carrying a folder in her hand. Having taken the interior light out of the truck, he silently opened his door and slipped out.

He was crouched down by the front fender, so she didn't notice him as she approached her car. She fumbled for her keys then turned when she heard him come up on her.

"Mrs. Calhoun." His voice was low and he stared into her eyes.

Dana looked up, eyes wide and took a step back; she felt something bad was going to happen. She started to scream when a hand covered her mouth and an arm circled her neck.

"Quiet! Don't make a fucking sound or you're dead." Dragging her over to the truck they were out of the glare of the street light. He squeezed her neck with his arm to make his point.

Her breath caught, she couldn't breathe! She frantically shook her head to get some air. The pressure around her neck eased and she took deep gulps. She was nearly in a total state of panic. She couldn't think. She wanted Bailey there.

"Don't hurt me, please. Take my money, my credit cards."

"You stupid bitch! I don't want your shit. I got a message to give your husband. Tell him to drop it. If he doesn't, you're going to be the one to pay."

"Drop what? I don't know what you mean." Her voice got louder, the panic breaking loose.

Making sure there wasn't anyone around who could hear, he released his arm from her neck.

"Thank you" She sucked air into her lungs.

He hit her on the bridge of her nose, a loud crack. She fell back and onto the truck. He grabbed her right arm and twisted it so hard Dana screamed out with pain. With her nose broken, the blood gushed out onto the asphalt. Using the toe of his boot, he kicked her in the side, knocking her to the ground. Streck got in the truck and drove away. It had taken about three minutes.

      *   *   *   *   *   *   *   *   *

When Dana hadn't shown by a quarter to eight, Bailey thought she was just going to be fashionably late. Then the doorbell rang. "Hey, you don't need to ring the doorbell for your own house." It rang two more times before he had the door open. Two policemen that Bailey casually knew were standing on the front stoop. "What going on, Jack, Kirk?" He didn't ask them in; he knew something was wrong.

One cop squared his shoulders. "Bailey, we've got to take you down to the station for some questioning."

"About what?"

"Dana's been assaulted. Now hold on a minute. She's in the hospital. We were told you two had been having problems and you hadn't been acting right lately."

"Oh, Christ. Take me up there."

"We gotta take you to the station, I said."

Bailey was having an adrenaline dump; he got tunnel vision and felt like he was choking. A feeling of murderous rage came over him. He stared at the two cops, clenching his fists.

"I'm going up to see Dana. Either you can take me and then we'll go to the P.D., or you better get the hell out of my way and call for some help. The choice is yours, make it now."

The two cops looked at each other. They knew of his reputation and had heard of Bailey's exploits. The two cops didn't think they wanted to try him. "Come on, we'll take you." They escorted him to the patrol car and put him in the back seat.

As they pulled into the hospital parking lot, Kirk turned his head to Bailey. "We won't cuff you, Bailey, but if you try anything shitty we'll hog-tie your ass and drag you out of there."

"Don't worry. If you guys think I did this, you're crazy. Hell, she was coming out to take me to dinner tonight. She was moving back in. Why would you think I'd do this?"

"Just between us, and I'll deny saying anything, the woman's abuse advocate — what's her name, Jenny Truman — said you had been drinking a lot and calling Dana all the time after she'd left. She thought you've been pretty pissed at times."

"For Christ's sake. What bullshit, but Dana will clear it up."

Their footsteps echoed down the hallway as they walked to the emergency room. Dana was in a corner bed with the privacy sheet pulled around. Bailey opened the edge and slipped in, the cops stayed out in the hall. His pulse skipped when he saw her. Dana's face was black and blue and swollen, her eyes were so bruised that he couldn't tell where they separated. Her nose was covered with a large bandage. She had a cast on her arm. There were cold packs surrounding her face, which added to the look of having a mask on. Her breathing seemed ragged with short breaths and a moan escaped from her lips.

The doctor came over to Bailey, "Are you the husband?" All Bailey could do was nod. He didn't trust himself to speak.

"Her nose is broken, we'll set it in the morning. Her arm has been severely traumatized; some son-of-a-bitch twisted it so far it stretched most of the ligaments. She's also been kicked in the side and one rib is cracked. What I want to know is — are you the son-of-a-bitch who did this to her?"

Tears ran down Bailey's face. He stood mute, shaking his head no.

"We've given her a sedative to make her sleep until morning. You won't be able to talk to her until then. Probably after we set her nose."

The two cops took him down to the police department and booked him. After he was fingerprinted and his mug shot taken, they asked him if he wanted to make a call.

"No, not now. Wait! Yeah, I do." He dialed the number and looked at the time on the office clock. 8:30 p.m. 7:30 in California. *Come on, answer.*

"Hello," a soft feminine voice answered. Linda had one of the nicest telephone voices Bailey had heard.

"Linda, this is Bailey, I need to talk to Jim." There was a pause while she apparently took the telephone to him.

"What're doing calling me up twice today, you after my woman?"

"Knock off the bullshit and listen. Somebody beat the hell out of Dana; she's in the hospital. The cops have me in jail until Dana can tell them I didn't do it."

"So why doesn't she tell them?"

"She's unconscious. Dana's hurt bad, Jim."

"You didn't do it, did you, Bailey? You're not that kind of prick."

"Hell no. Look Jim, can you fly down here? I need help and there isn't anyone else I trust. I want to warn you, you could get hurt, royally."

"Yeah, I can do it. I'll get on the first flight to Denver and be in Rawlins before you know it."

"What about your business?"

"Linda can run it. She does better than me anyway. Wiggles her ass in their faces and they sign on the dotted line. She makes twice as much on a car as I do. Besides, I need a break; I've been selling shit cars to shit people for too long. See you in the morning sometime."

Bailey was put in a cell by himself. He laid down on the cot and wondered how this played in with everything. He didn't believe in coincidences like this. He got up and went over to the cell door. "Hey, Kirk. Will you call the Davison's and ask them to put Callie in the yard? Thanks."

*　　*　　*　　*　　*　　*　　*　　*　　*

Streck drove down two blocks then parked his truck. He trotted back to the library and crept into the alley across the street. Someone had already found the bitch and was kneeling down by her. He could hear the sirens then ducked down as the first cop car pulled up. Seconds later, red lights flashing, the ambulance screeched to a halt. He watched the attendants hover over her then put her on a gurney and load her into the back. Tires squealing, siren blaring, it raced off into the night.

Calhoun would of shit himself if I'd raped her. Back in his truck and in a mood to celebrate, he bought a pint of Old Crow and a six pack of Bud. When he got to his room he poured a water glass full of whiskey, then laid on the bed with his beer and Old Crow on the table and proceeded to get drunk while relishing the memory of her struggle.

*　　*　　*　　*　　*　　*　　*　　*　　*

Bailey didn't sleep that night; he kept envisioning Dana's battered face with eyes black and swollen shut and the cast on her arm. He was fed breakfast at seven but just drank the coffee. Being Sunday, there wouldn't be court until the next day when his bond should be set. When Dana came around and was able to tell them Bailey didn't beat her up, he should be out sooner.

Unfortunately, it wasn't going to happen that day. The doctor kept her sedated all day Sunday and Jim had called and wasn't able to get to Rawlins until Monday morning. *Goddamn airlines.* Bailey spent all Sunday in the cell. The cops did let him call the hospital several times to check on Dana. A little before eleven Monday morning, he heard a disturbance in the main station.

"I don't give a shit, call the City Attorney and have him release Bailey. You were there, goddammit. You heard her say he didn't do it. If I have to call a lawyer, I'll make sure to have your ass." Jim walked in with a serious expression on his face. "Christ, Bailey, what happened?"

They could hear the cops talking to the City Attorney on the phone.

A few minutes later the jailer came in and opened the cell door. "The City Attorney says we can let you go since your wife said it wasn't you." He stood by the door waiting for Bailey to gather his things and leave. "You finished raising hell now? It wasn't my fault; I was just doing my job," the jailor said.

"Yeah, that's always a good excuse," Jim shot back.

"I want to go to the hospital after I shower and change." Bailey said. He got in Jim's rental car and slumped down in the seat, closing his eyes.

They didn't talk on the way to the house and when they pulled into the driveway and stopped, Bailey got out and went into the back yard. He ignored Callie jumping on him and put some food into her bowl. Jim followed him into the house.

"Come on, Bailey, yell, knock some holes in the wall. Do something, you got to let it out."

Jim sat down while Bailey took a shower. He saw Bailey's notebook and flipped through some of the pages. He noticed the house looked like it was waiting for a visitor, everything picked up and put away. It was hard for him to believe it was thirty-six hours ago when Bailey called him in such a great mood. He was pissed he couldn't bring a gun because of flying to Rawlins. Bailey always said Jim liked to collect guns. He had enough to hold a small army of Democrats at bay if they passed a gun bill and tried getting his. Being a businessman, he was a dyed-in-the-wool, one hundred per cent, get rid of the social programs, Republican. Bailey was half-and-half and they used to have some hellacious arguments over politics. Jim would get so mad he would usually end up saying, "Oh fuck you, Bailey, you liberal Democratic do-gooder." Eventually they would have a couple of beers and go on to solve the remaining problems of America and the world.

Bailey came out of the bedroom dressed in clean clothes and looking like someone had stepped on his grave.

"Hey, thanks for coming." Bailey's voice sent a chill up McConroy's spine. "I'm going to get the son-of-a-bitch who did this and tear his heart out." He walked over to the living room window and stared out over the town.

"Out of all the things I've done, there's been a lot I haven't been proud of——the shit I did in Vietnam, watching friends die over there, but nothing has ever made me feel like this. I want to watch somebody die and have them know I killed them." He shook himself then looked like he hadn't realized where he was. "Let's go see Dana."

They got in Jim's rental, a black Lincoln (I'm not driving no stinking Taurus) and drove up to the hospital. They parked in the back, where the employees parked their cars and went through the entrance to the emergency room. They rode the elevator to the second floor and entered her room.

Dana was lying on her back with bandages around her face, covering her nose. The arm in the cast was lying across her stomach, and it looked like she had a chest strap on for the cracked rib. One eye opened and she lifted her hand to Bailey while tears started running down her cheeks.

"Oh, Bailey. God, I was so scared, I thought he was going to kill me." Her crying increased. Jim, looking uncomfortable, patted her hand and left the room. Bailey put his arms around her as gently as possible. She flinched when he grazed her side.

"Tell me what happened, Dana, but go as slow as you need to. You're safe." His voice was just above a whisper.

"He grabbed me when I was going to get in the car. He had his arm around my throat and I couldn't breathe. At first I thought he was going to rape me, but he just kept my neck in his arm. God, he was strong. I told him to take my money." She shuddered as the memories were becoming more intense.

131

"I think I'm going to throw up." He helped her out of the bed then she went into the bathroom and vomited into the toilet. He rinsed a washcloth out and wiped her mouth as gently as he could. She slowly got back into the hospital bed.

"You don't have to talk anymore. Why don't you rest and I'll come back later and you can finish."

"No. I need to finish telling you. He told me he didn't want my money. He had a message to give you."

"Give me?"

"He said to drop what you're doing or I'm going to pay or something like that, then he hit me; I didn't remember anything until this morning."

"What'd he look like, do you remember?"

"All that I remember is he was big and strong. Not as tall as you, but he was heavier. He had dark hair and a beard, but not a long one. And he smelled like he hadn't bathed in days. I can't remember anymore, Bailey. I'm sorry." The tears started again and he held her.

"I'm going to talk to the doctor and find out when you can leave here, and then I'm going to get you out of Rawlins until this is over. Maybe fly you out to Linda's, have you stay there." Bailey told her.

Dana shook her head, "no."

"At least I know you'll be safe, then I won't have to worry about you while I'm going after these pricks. I'm going to need Jim to cover my back and he can't do that and watch you. No one else is going to do help us, Dana, so quit tell me no."

"Bailey, it's not like Linda won't welcome me, but dammit, I'm not going to let myself get chased out of town by that bastard. Give me a gun and I'll lock myself in the basement with Callie, but I'm not leaving."

She had a resolved look and said, "I not going to leave you. I'm staying, Bailey. I'll carry a gun. Damn him, he's not going to scare me out." The pride Bailey felt made him swell his chest; this was his partner, his soul mate.

"All right. I'm going to see if I can get some protection for you until you can come home, is that okay?" He had a bit of a grin starting.

"Yes. I'm not going to run away, but I'm still scared of him."

He approached the doctor at the nurse's station and asked how long Dana would have to stay.

The doctor looked at his notes. "Probably another day or two. I want to keep her quiet, make sure she hasn't had any head injuries that we are unaware of. Let's say Tuesday evening, unless she wants to stay longer."

Bailey thanked him and shook his hand. He felt as if he owed the doctor a lot more than the bill he'd get. He and Jim got into the Lincoln.

"What's next?" Jim asked as he put the key in and started the car.

"Take me to the office, I want to see if Williams and Travis are there; I'm going to have a little talk with them."

Chapter Seventeen

When Calvin picked the phone up after the second ring, he knew it wasn't going to be good news. There hadn't been much good news lately.

"Hello." He could hear the hum over the wires.

"This is Streck. I got the woman; she's in the hospital. I told her to tell Calhoun to drop it." His flat monotone drawled out. "I'm gonna need some money. I also need a cell phone because I'm on the move now."

"How much do you need?"

"Five thousand, twenties and fifties." Streck said.

"Five thousand! God, I'll have to go to the bank for that much."

The thought of possibly having to meet Streck face to face upset Calvin. He had reasoned the whole messy business could be taken care of over the phone, not in person.

"Meet me with the money and the cell down at the river. I think they call it the Dugway Picnic Grounds. Be there around seven tonight. We on the right track?"

"Yes, yes. It will be safe, won't it? No chance of Calhoun following you down there?" Calvin could feel the sweat dripping down his sides as he pulled his handkerchief out of his pocket and mopped his forehead. He seemed to break into a sweat with very little coaxing lately.

"Don't worry, Knight. If he does, he won't be coming back."

*   *   *   *   *   *   *   *   *

Streck hung the phone up and called the Idle Hours Bar in Denver. When it was answered he asked if Lynch or Gomez had been checking for messages. He was told they had come in or called the last couple of days. Streck gave the bartender a message for them. "Tell them to come back tonight, stay at the same place, same name. I'll get ahold of them tomorrow. Tell them it's payday."

He wanted to find Calhoun and follow him around a bit, see how he moved. Confronting Calhoun was getting to be an obsession. Streck knew he could take him. Just like he fucked Calhoun's wife up. But it would be more of a challenge.

While Streck had seen Calhoun talking to that old fart out in the boonies last week through his binoculars, he was able to see him close up in town a few days later. He had been in the post office when it was snowing out and Calhoun had come in and mailed a package, then stood around the door. He'd wanted to take him out right there, but the timing wasn't right. Following him, he sat at the counter at the Square Shooters when Calhoun and his wife came in for lunch. He'd frozen his ass off waiting outside the library, thinking maybe they weren't coming out, but they did. Yeah, he knew what Calhoun looked like. He almost rubbed his hands together in anticipation.

Chapter Eighteen

Bailey and Jim drove down to the BLM office on Fifth and Cedar. He told Jim to hang around by his car and he took the stairs up to the second floor and walked in the office.

"Dora, where's Travis?" He had asked as he was walking toward his desk. "Where're my papers?"

No one was sitting at Travis's desk. Williams came strutting over from his office.

"Calhoun, I'm informing you that you're under suspension. You're to leave here immediately and you will be notified when to attend your hearing."

"What the hell are you talking about, John? Suspended for what?" He had turned to face Williams and was gripping the desk so hard his knuckles were white.

"You were arrested and thrown in jail for assault. It hasn't gone to trial yet, so you're suspended until the case is disposed."

"That's bullshit, John. They never filed charges. Dana told them it wasn't me, that's why I'm here and not in jail."

"There's nothing I can do about it. This has to do with domestic violence, and you know how the government feels about that. Any change will have to come out of Cheyenne. Until then, you will not act in any manner as an agent of the Bureau of Land Management. Is that understood?" Williams bristled, as he stood a little taller.

Bailey's face turned crimson. "Fuck you, Williams, I quit." Williams jumped back as he pushed by him. Looking over at Dora, Bailey saw her staring intently at her computer screen.

He stomped down the stairs and met Jim on the sidewalk outside the building.

"Let's walk over to the café and get some breakfast." Jim fell in beside him.

"So what's going on?" Jim asked, already puffing after a half a block. He opened the door and he and Bailey went to a back booth and sat down. Out of habit, Bailey sat so he could see the door.

"They suspended me, I quit. Williams is in on it. Knight has to be involved also, and so's Knight's kid, Travis. I still don't understand what the hell is going on. Wild horses are killed in the Red Desert, then here. Both by the same guns. Knight has tried to renew a lease on the refuge. Can't do it. Some more horses are killed and yet they're left lying where anyone could find them. Dana's beaten up and told to tell me to drop it. What do you think? You were always a sneaky bastard."

Jim had been doodling on the napkin, "Nothing new from Rock Springs? I mean, no more dead horses found? You told me a Deputy there was handling the case and had told you what they had." Bailey was nodding his head yes.

Jim continued. "You got one incident in Rock Springs and at least two here. Rock Springs was state land; the federal refuge is here. No more horse killings around Rock Springs. Then there's lease applications, Dana getting beat up, you suspended/quit, an exploration company that you said had a prior lease before the refuge was set up. I think———," Jim paused then drank some coffee, "I think that the horses at Rock Springs were a red herring. I don't know why, but it sounds like it was either a trial run or they wanted both places to seem like random acts of killings."

"I'm impressed with your powers of deduction, Jim, but what good would it do them when it's a refuge? Dammit, they can't get a lease on it." Bailey was craning his neck and looking out the window.

"What the hell are you looking at, Bailey?" Jim turned and looked.

"That shitty green truck across the street. I've just been seeing it around lately. Looks like some kids painted it with spray paint. Hey, Dana had said she had something interesting for me on the refuge bill. Christ, I forgot all about it. We'll ask her when we go up later. Let's get out of here and go see if Calvin's at the Golden Eagle." Leaving some money on the table, they left the café and went back to Jim's car.

The Golden Eagle Gas and Exploration Company was situated near the airport, east of town. As they were turning onto the frontage road that would take them in to the yard, they saw Calvin in his white Cadillac turning onto the highway going west into town.

"Well, turn around, my man, let's see if we can follow him," Bailey said.

Jim eased the Lincoln into a u-turn then ran the stop sign as he turned west. He gunned it until he came to within six cars of Knight.

Turning at Fourth Street, Knight drove into the parking lot of the Rocky Mountain Industrial Bank. He took up two parking spaces and rapidly walked in the front door. Jim and Bailey pulled over on the side street and waited for him to come back. After ten minutes Knight came out and left in his car. His tires squealed as he accelerated down the street. The Lincoln pulled out and followed at a discreet distance. Knight drove directly back to the Golden Eagle where he parked his car in the large garage and went in the building. Bailey told Jim to pull up in front of the office building. He got out of the car, opened the lobby door, and approached the receptionist.

"May I help you, Sir?" She looked at him expectantly.

"Yes, I'd like to see Calvin, please." Bailey tried making it sound as if they were old friends.

It didn't work. "May I have your name and I'll see if Mr. Knight is in."

"Bailey Calhoun, he's expecting me." He gave her a big smile; he knew he had won her over.

"I'm sorry, Mr. Calhoun, Mr. Knight is out of the office for the rest of the day. If you care to leave a message or number, I'm sure he'll get back to you in the morning."

"That's okay, I'll just see him at his house." Bailey left the office and climbed into the car. "The bastard's hiding up there. They said he's gone for the day. We'll see if I shook him up. I told her to tell him I'd see him at his house."

Jim elbowed him. "Isn't that the green pickup you saw, up on the hill there?" Jim was pointing to a hill by the railroad tracks across the highway. "Looks like the same one that was by the café."

"Yeah, it does. I wish this was a four-wheel drive, we'd find out who the hell that is. Let's just sit here for a minute and let Knight stew, knowing we're out here. Maybe the guy in the truck will do something."

After ten minutes they left. When they pulled onto the highway the truck was no longer on the hill.

Bailey had Jim take them to his house where he got on the telephone to the police department. "Lt. Durning, please. Yes, I'll hold——— Brian, would you be able to have someone posted at the hospital for the next twenty-four hours to watch Dana? Yeah, the guy told her he would get her again. I need the time to get things ready for her, and I'm involved in a case that I just need a day or so to finish——— That's bullshit, Brian. It's an assault case with a chance of happening again——— No, thanks just the same."

Bailey threw the phone down. "Goddamn him! He says there's not enough evidence to warrant a guard. Jim, I need you to stay up there with her. I've got to find Travis and maybe beat some truth out of him."

"No problem, that's what I'm here for. Once we get her home, we can work out a plan to cover her."

Bailey went in his shop and came out with a Smith and Wesson .38 snub nose. Giving it to Jim, he said, "If you have to shoot more than five feet away, you're screwed."

Bailey had his Rugar P-90 in his hand. It was a stainless steel, double action .45 caliber. The pistol held seven rounds in the clip and one in the chamber. It felt good in his hand.

"About all we need now are a Huey and some gooks shooting at us." Jim said. He pocketed the .38 and looked hard at Bailey.

"Are you okay? I got a feeling that shit's going to hit the fan."

Bailey smiled, "Yeah, and somebody better be out of range."

*   *   *   *   *   *   *   *   *

Streck watched them in the café then followed them to the Golden Eagle, where he turned to the south and climbed the hill with his truck. He turned around by the railroad tracks and faced the Golden Eagle below him and to the north.

He watched the Lincoln take off behind Knight. Feeling they would be back, he stayed where he was. A bit over twenty minutes had passed when Knight came back, the Lincoln a discreet distance behind. He watched the Lincoln pull up to the office and Calhoun get out. Streck pulled his binoculars from the case and as he focused the lenses, Jim's profile came into view. *So he's got some help. This will be interesting.*

When Calhoun came out and got in the car, he thought he might have been seen. He watched them for a minute then put the truck in gear and followed the tracks east until he came to Sinclair. He got off the track right-of-way and drove up Eighth Street and stopped by the park. He saw a pay phone and put some coins in as he dialed the number.

Calvin felt true fear when his private line rang. Once, twice, three times and he finally picked it up. "Yes?"

"Looks like Calhoun's after you."

"I know, what am I going to do? God, I'm scared to leave in case he sees me."

"Did you get the money and phone?"

"Yes, I've got both. Jesus, my hand is trembling so hard I can hardly hold onto the phone. Can you help me, Streck? Protect me and I'll give you another $2500."

"Listen, you stay holed up in your office until tonight, then meet me at the river. I'll be around and if they try anything, I'll take them out."

"You're not worried about Calhoun?"

"Shit, no, he'll just be another notch on the ol' pistola. I also got some associates coming in tonight to finish the job out north."

"That would make a big difference. Get this damn thing over with. I don't know how much more I can take." Calvin said.

"I've also got the tractor trailer with the backhoe parked out by Three Forks." Calvin said. "You need to bury those horses that are in the canyon. Fritz Meade will be there tomorrow night around seven, the sun will be down then. What are you going to do after you bury them?"

Streck didn't want to really tell him, but he thought it'd help the bastard settle down if he knew everything was going to be taken care of.

"A couple miles down is a small canyon. I'm gonna dig a ditch at the back of it then run some horses in and leave them. They oughta be settled down after a couple of days; then we'll kill 'em and bury them. Nobody will find them." Streck paused for a moment. "What I wanna do, is to get Calhoun up there. I think I'm gonna get his old lady again too. Really fuck her up this time. Maybe I'll do that first."

"Why on earth do you want to get Calhoun? Let's just get this done."

"Don't you worry about that, Knight. Seems like everybody thinks he's so goddamn tough; hell, you're all scared of him. I want Calhoun to know I can take him. I want him to know that before I kill him."

*   *   *   *   *   *   *   *   *

Jim left for the hospital after bitching about what a shitty little gun Bailey had given him. Bailey picked up the phone and dialed Mike Hampston's number in Denver.

"Special Agent Hampston," he answered.

"Christ, I'm glad you're there. This is Bailey, Mike, you find out anything for me yet?"

"Hey, where's the kiss before the sex?"

"Things are snowballing, Mike. Dana got the shit beat out of her and the guy told her to tell me to drop what I was doing. What do you have?"

"Jesus, Bailey, is she okay?" The concern in his voice was evident.

"She's gonna be. I got Jim McConroy to come back and help me. I think we'll stash her somewhere until we get this done, one way or another."

"Bring her down here; she can stay at my place or we can get her a hotel."

"Thanks, Mike, but you know how stubborn those women can get. She says no one is going to run her out and she's staying even if it means packing a gun." He smiled when he thought of Dana saying that, even though the resolved look in her eyes made her wince.

"Yeah, that sounds like her. Nothing much about Williams in Bozeman. The time he was there he was known as a ladder climber. Screwed a couple guys over to get an advancement. That's what got him to Vegas. I did some checking with a friend in the FBI down there, and when I mentioned the Rawlins BLM he got interested. An informant was just pulled out that was chummy in the mob until some dumb shit squealed on him. He wouldn't tell me what all was going on, but he promised to check into some things."

"Why wouldn't they have done something by now? Williams has been here a couple of years." Bailey asked.

"I guess the Feds didn't want to give anything away until they're ready to get an indictment. But listen, if Dana getting beaten up has anything to do with this stuff, I'll call my buddy back and get him going. If I get something that will help you in the next day or so I'll call. If you don't hear from me by Wednesday night, call me. I might have to drive down to Alamosa to do some interviewing on that counterfeiting case I was telling you about Thursday. Grab a pen and I'll give you my pager number." He rattled off his pager number and cell number to Bailey.

"If there's any way I can come down and help, I will, Bailey, but we're

143

getting our asses run right now."

"Don't worry, Mike. I appreciate what you're doing. I've tried getting the U.S. Marshall's office involved, but everyone's too busy to put some dead wild horses very high on their agendas. But, I don't blame them; it's not like I've got some rock-hard evidence of a huge conspiracy. If you can find anything out from the fed's snitch pertaining to Williams, that might be the kicker."

The phone rang as soon as Bailey had hung it up. "Yeah——— Jim, what's up?"

"I was going to ask Dana about the information she had for you on the refuge, but they have her sedated. I guess she was hurting pretty bad so they gave her a shot of something. She's gonna be out a couple of hours. You come up with anything?"

"Maybe; I talked to a Secret Service friend of mine in Denver and he might have something interesting on Williams in a day or two. If he does, I'm going nail his ass to the wall. I'll be up in a couple of hours and give you a break," Bailey said.

"Only if you want to; I think you oughta get some sleep. I called Linda and she's made us a ton of money today. Sold three cars. Christ, I've been trying to dump those three for two months."

"I'll lie down for a while, then I'm going try and find Travis. I should be up at the hospital around eight tonight." He sounded weary to himself; he knew Jim was right about getting some sleep.

Lying down on the couch he knew he wouldn't be able to sleep. He woke up three hours later. Brushing his teeth then getting his Ruger, he went to his truck. Sticking the gun under the console, he went in search of Travis. He cruised the parking lots of the "in" bars but didn't see Travis's dark blue Tahoe. Pulling up to Travis's house, the lights were on and his Tahoe was parked in front of the garage.

He knocked on the door. He could hear country music playing on the stereo and Travis came up to the door.

"Hey, Calhoun, what's going on?" He took a sip out of his beer but didn't open the screen door.

Bailey yanked the door open and grabbed Travis's throat with one hand, squeezing with his thumb and fingers. Pushing him in the house, he slammed Travis against the living room wall and kicked the beer bottle that Travis had dropped out of the way. Travis pawed at the hand around his throat. Bailey reached down and grabbed his balls. "You want to use these again, Travis, you better come up with some right answers. Now quit fighting me."

Travis's eyes were big and he nodded. Bailey loosened his grip.

"What the hell are you doing, Calhoun. I can have your ass arrested." He shook Bailey's hand off and shrank against the wall.

"Jesus, that hurt." He rubbed his crotch, then looked at Bailey and quit.

"You said you found twelve horses that had died from winterkill. That right?"

"Yeah ... yeah, that's right. Out by Ridley's Ridge."

Bailey moved in closer until he was inches from Travis's face. "You lying sack of shit. The horses had all been shot. There's another twenty down in the box canyon. They were shot and killed too. Now quit lying to me, Travis, or I'm going to beat you within an inch of your life." Bailey slapped him across the nose.

Travis's eyes welled up with tears from the sting of the slap. He put his hands up.

"Bailey, I didn't go down and look at the horses. I saw them lying down there in the gulch and it stunk so bad, I puked. I figured they'd died from the winter and I didn't want to screw with them. What the fuck is going on?"

Bailey had taken his hands off Travis. That would be something Travis would have done, not check the horses then blame it on winterkill.

"What about the stuff on your desk having to do with Frank?"

"I don't like the old bastard. He's always giving me shit so I noticed his tags were expired. I was going to cite him, you know, throw a screw to him." Travis was frowning, knowing that Calhoun didn't think much of him, particularly then.

145

"All right, Travis, I'm going leave it at that right now. I think your father and Williams are involved in something that resulted in Dana getting beat to shit. If I find out that you lied to me, there won't be anywhere safe to hide. You understand?"

"I'm telling you the truth, Bailey. And believe me, there's nothing I would do that would hurt Dana. I swear to God." He watched Bailey nod his head and leave.

Chapter Nineteen

Calvin stayed locked in his office until after the sun had gone down. Everyone had left several hours ago. He didn't want to take his Cadillac to the river when he met Streck so he decided to take the back streets home and get Margo's Land Rover.

He left the company garage with his lights off and drove towards the airport. He turned and drove through the industrial addition, crossed the highway, and worked his way up to his home. He circled the block first to see if Calhoun's pickup or the black Lincoln he'd seen earlier with Calhoun in it was parked on the streets. When he was reasonably sure no one was waiting for him he parked in the garage and closed the door. Margo's Land Rover was angled in to the side. Knight started it up and left by the same route he had just come from.

When he turned at the junction to the river he looked around to see if he could see Streck or anyone, but he didn't. Five miles later he pulled into the Dugway Picnic Grounds. No one was around. He started to panic when a green truck pulled in. Streck parked behind him and got out. He looked in the back seat as he approached Knight, who was rolling the driver's window down.

"You got the money and phone?" Streck asked standing back from the window.

Calvin said he did and started to open the car door.

"You don't need to get out. Just give me the stuff."

"All right, here." He handed Streck the envelope with the money in it and a small cell phone. "The number is taped on the front."

"Okay. I've got something going on so I'll talk to you later, Knight." Dismissing Calvin, Streck climbed in his truck, started it up and turned in the direction of town.

Calvin rolled his window up thinking, *he made me break out in a sweat with three sentences.* He turned around and followed Streck's receding tail-lights back to Rawlins.

    *   *   *   *   *   *   *   *   *

Travis came into the house and found his mother drunk in the living room. She had a magazine lying in her lap and her head hanging down onto her chest.

Gently lifting her arm, Travis spoke to her, "Come on, Mom, let's get you to bed." He helped her to her feet where she swayed a little then put his arm around her waist and helped her up the stairs to her bedroom. He pulled the covers back and she got into the bed, pushing her shoes off with her feet. He covered her up and kissed her cheek.

She put her arms around him and with a voice slurred from the half bottle of whiskey, said, "Travie, you never come around anymore. Sit with me until I go to sleep."

"Okay, Mom, lay back and close your eyes. Goodnight." She sighed and held on to his arm.

He heard his father come in just as the phone rang.

"Hello. Streck——why are you calling me now? I just gave you the money and cell phone." The normal tone of Calvin wasn't frightened, like it was now.

Travis silently picked his mother's phone up and held it to his ear, covering the mouthpiece with his hand.

"I tried calling you at your office; when you didn't answer I figured you went home." Streck said into the phone.

"We're gonna do the last of the horses in a couple of nights. I want you out there." Streck's voice was challenging.

"Me? Why the hell do you want me out there, for Christ sake?"

Travis could hear the fear in Calvin's voice. Something new.

"Cause then you can't fuck me over. You're gonna shoot a couple of them yourself."

"No...no. I'm not going to do this. You take care of it and I'll pay you more," Calvin pleaded.

"It's costing you more anyway, Calvin. You're gonna meet us when I tell you to, or you might be next after I take care of Calhoun."

"I'm going to call..."

"Shut your face. I don't think your friend is going to help you. I already told him what I was gonna do and he liked it. In fact he said you needed to be taking some of the risk. So call whoever you want, but you better come when I tell you. Got it?"

Calvin spoke in a rush of panicked words. "You've got to get this over with. I don't know how much more of this I can take." The connection was broken and he heard his father hang up.

Calhoun was right, the old man is in it, up to his ass, I'd say, Travis thought.

Travis and Calvin had never been close. Calvin demanded perfection from the boy since he had been a child.

"Travis, we have a place in society here, so you're going to walk the line. You had better not do anything that will ever embarrass me," Calvin would harp.

One time Travis had stayed out past his curfew, drinking with some of his friends when Calvin caught him. He didn't say anything, just motioned for Travis to get into the car. When they got home, Calvin took a belt strap and beat him so bad he had to miss school for a week. His mother had tried interfering for him, but Calvin slapped the shit out of her. He told her she was nothing without him and if she didn't shut up and go to the house, she'd be gone along with the loss of the money and power.

That was when she started drinking. First a few with her friends before dinner, then it progressed to starting around noon and passing out in the early evening.

Travis accepted his father's discipline, but he hated him for what he did to his mother.

He gently put the phone on its cradle and wondered how he was going to leave the house without Calvin hearing him. That was settled when he heard the Land Rover back out of the garage and drive off into the night.

He had walked to his parents' house, needing to clear his head after Bailey had confronted him. At first, he couldn't see how Calhoun could have thought he was involved, but after Bailey had told him what all had happened, then hearing his father on the phone, he understood. He needed to find Bailey and tell him what he had heard. Walking east and down a hill Travis came to his house. It was a small bungalow located near the fairgrounds with a patio between the garage and house.

He went in and tried to call Calhoun, but no one answered. Next he tried the hospital, asking for Dana's room.

It rang for several times before it was answered.

"Hello." A male voice he didn't recognize.

"I'm trying to call Dana Calhoun's room. Is this it?"

"Who's calling?"

"This is Travis Knight, I need to talk to Bailey, it's important."

"He's not here. Give me your number and I'll have him call you."

"Tell him to call me at my house. Call or come by. Like I said, it's important."

*   *   *   *   *   *   *   *   *

Jim wrote the number down and saw his reflection in the windows. *Something is breaking loose, I think the party's starting.*

Bailey came in the room about fifteen minutes later. "How's everything going? Dana's still under?"

"Yeah, some guy called, said his name was Travis Knight, wants you to call or go to his house. He said it's important."

"I wonder what the hell he wants. I choked him down a little and got some answers, but not the ones I thought."

Jim stretched and said, "Let me run over and grab a burger, I'll be right back, then you can go see him."

"Go, take your time. Knight can wait a bit, or maybe I'll call him. No, I'll go to his house; if you look someone in the eye it's harder for them to lie to you."

Jim left the hospital and drove down to Wendy's on the east end of town. He ordered at the drive-through window, not wanting to take much time so Bailey could go see what Knight had to say. He picked his order up and was back in Dana's room thirty minutes after he'd left.

"Jim, dammit, I told you to take your time." He caught the sack that was thrown him.

"I hope you like double burgers and fries; I didn't think you'd eaten yet."

Bailey opened the sack and bit into a burger. "Jesus, this tastes good. I didn't know I was so hungry."

The doctor came in on his evening rounds and checked Dana. "She's been in a lot of pain from her injuries; I think we'll keep her at least through tomorrow. If she's feeling better and is ambulatory, we'll look at releasing her late tomorrow. She should be waking up in an hour or two."

"Thanks, Doc," replied Bailey. "One of us will be staying with her, do you have a problem with that?"

"No, not at all. I'll look in on her during my morning rounds." He left the room and his footsteps echoed as he hurried down the hall.

"Jim, let me go talk to Travis, then I'll come and stay the night. You can stay at the house and come up when you're ready in the morning."

"Okay, Bailey. Take your time, there hasn't been anything out of the ordinary."

"Travis." Bailey spoke into his cell phone, "I'm on my way down to your house, I'll be there in ten minutes."

He circled the block twice, seeing if there were any cars or trucks that seemed out of place, then pulled into Travis's driveway again.

Standing to the side of the door, he knocked. His pistol was snuggled to his side, under his jacket. Travis opened the door and held it open, motioning for Bailey to enter. Scanning the front room, he walked in.

"You still don't trust me, do you?"

"Trust has to be earned, Travis," Bailey countered.

"I heard Dad on the phone tonight at his house, talking to a guy named Streck. He told Dad to meet him."

"When, did he say?"

Travis shrugged his shoulders. "Sometime in the next couple of days, I think. I'm not sure. This Streck said they were gonna kill some more horses. He said Dad could call his friend and it wouldn't do any good. They wanted Dad doing some of the dirty work."

"Where's Calvin now?"

"I don't know. He took the Land Rover and left."

"Are you sure it wasn't tonight, Travis?" Bailey was walking back and forth across the living room.

"Yeah, I'm sure. Said in a couple of nights."

"All right, Travis, I'm going to let you earn my trust. You have to find out when and where Streck and Calvin are going to kill the horses. Here's my cell phone number; let me know as soon as you find out. And———thanks."

When Bailey left this time, he felt the end was coming soon.

Chapter Twenty

Calvin knew the situation was getting out of hand, but it was too late to get out. He had to see it through, no matter what happened. His cabin was near the little mountain town of Ryan Park. After an hour and fifteen minutes of driving, he pulled into his gate.

The cabin sat on three wooded acres facing south. He took the key from the porch roof eve and unlocked the front door, turning the lights on as he came into the main room. Going to a cupboard by the kitchen he opened one of the cupboard doors and brought out a glass and bottle of Black Velvet. He poured a glass full and drank half, then refilled the glass. Another couple of swallows and he relaxed as he sat in a large leather easy chair. Calvin thought of his conversation with John Williams earlier that day.

"Calvin," Williams sat down in front of the desk, taking a small sip of his drink, "We have to get this ironed out. I pushed my limits by suspending Calhoun. I need to have the job offer in writing by Wednesday."

Knight took a swallow of his whiskey while listening to Williams. "John, things are in a turmoil right now. Can't this wait until after the lease is in effect?"

"Frankly, no. It wouldn't look appropriate if I started to work for you after the refuge reverted back. It would be much better to start as a lobbyist prior to the Golden Eagle getting the lease rights. If not it would look like preferential treatment had been given." Williams crossed his legs and pulled a notebook out of his pocket. "I think that a salary of $125,000 a year plus living expenses to start would be in the ball park, don't you?"

Knight turned his chair to look out the window. With his back to Williams he said, "John, right now isn't a good time. I have a lot of irons in the fire; we should talk about this at the end of the month."

Williams stood and walked over to the window, looking out toward Elk Mountain, "Calvin, no. I don't like to push, you know that. I want a letter Wednesday with the job offer and salary requirements I gave you, to be effective in two weeks. That's the maximum time I will give you. There should be a contract for five years minimum and guaranteed cost of living increases with annual raises 3% above the current inflation rate with the letter. Don't take me wrong. I'm not threatening, but if I don't have this by noon, day after tomorrow, the lease proposal might be lost in the paperwork. It's ready to go now, but it could still be lost. Do you understand me?" He turned to look at Knight as he said the last sentence.

"John, I understand completely. Welcome aboard Golden Eagle Gas and Exploration. As our Washington lobbyist." Calvin stood up and shook his hand.

The triumph on Williams's face made it look as if it were glowing. "Thank you, Calvin. Let's have one more drink to toast our relationship."

After pouring more whiskey into their glasses, Calvin lifted his glass in a mock salute.

"Here's to us, John. May our future be long and prosperous." They both took a sip and Knight said,

"John, I'm going to have to get this paper work done for you, so if you'll excuse me, I'll get started."

"Certainly. I'm looking forward to this relationship." He put on his jacket and hat and left the office.

The *pompous little bastard picked a bad time*, Calvin thought. He wondered how long it would take before Williams started turning the screws with more demands. *He'll want my company in six months*. Draining the glass, he refilled it once more to the top. Another long swallow and he took his cell phone and dialed.

Chapter Twenty-one

Bailey told Jim to go home and sleep. "Make sure to drive by the house first, see if any thing looks out of whack."

Jim left and drove east on Spruce Street checking the parking lots of the motels, hoping he would see the shitty green crew cab. When he got to Third Street he turned north and after several minutes drove by Bailey's house. Not seeing anything out of the ordinary, he made a u-turn and parked in the driveway.

The dog barked as he went in the front door but quieted down when Jim let her in the house. After a few perfunctory smells, she apparently remembered him and followed him to the refrigerator as he got himself a beer and gave her a piece of chicken. She sat at his feet eating the chicken as he drank his beer.

"Well girl, I know there hasn't been anyone in this house with a bad ass like you guarding it." He petted her head and turned on the TV.

The news was just ending. "As of yet the suspect in the Patsy Mae Brinkman murder hasn't been apprehended." He turned the channel and started watching a rerun of X-Files as he finished the first beer and popped open another.

*   *   *   *   *   *   *   *   *

Stroking Dana's face, Bailey felt his anger building. He thought that the person that did this was really an animal, a rabid animal. *You took care of something rabid by killing it before it bit you.* That's what Bailey was going to do, kill it before it bit him.

He settled down in the reclining chair. The nurses had brought some blankets and a pillow in for him. He put his pistol on the floor by the wall and slept fitfully through the night. Several times, Dana cried out and awakened him. He'd sit by her and cool her head with a wet wash cloth. A nurse came in around three in the morning and gave her a shot after Bailey rang them. Dana had started to moan and then sat up in the bed, eyes wide open, not knowing where she was. Not recognizing Bailey, she tried flaying with her fists but he held her close so she couldn't harm herself. She finally settled down and slept the rest of the night.

At 8:00 a.m., the doctor came in and examined her. "She's better, physically, believe it or not, but she's exhausted. Let's leave her the rest of the day and if she sleeps and doesn't have much pain, we'll release her this afternoon or early evening." He looked at Bailey to see if he agreed.

"That's fine, Dr. Rivers, I appreciate your attention to Dana."

"I know your friend is staying here with her also, but call the front desk later and I'll leave word when she can probably go." He waved as he left the room.

Drinking coffee and holding an extra cup, Jim walked in and handed one to Bailey.

"Here, why don't you leave and I'll stay the rest of the day?"

"That really sounds good; I'm going take you up on it. The doctor said he'll let the front desk know when Dana can leave, so we can check with them later."

He picked his gun up and held it out to Jim. "Take it, I know you don't like that snubnose."

"Naaaah, this is a piece of shit, but it'll work for now. You decide we're gonna have a shoot out, then I'll change." He took the Smith & Wesson out of his pocket and put it in the drawer under the bed tray.

When Bailey got home he called Rudy Maes in Rock Springs.

"Deputy Maes, can I help you?"

"Rudy, this is Bailey. I've got some interesting things going on."

"What do you got, Bailey?"

"To start off, my wife was beaten and given a message for me to back off or she'd get it worse."

"Jesus, do you know who did it?"

"Yeah, I got an idea, or at least who gave the order. I found out that there is going be some more horses killed in a couple of days and the owner of the Golden Eagle Gas and Exploration is going to be doing some of the shooting. There's someone that's supposed to find out when it's going to happen and let me know."

"Bailey, that's great. That'll be a hell of a tag. Congratulations."

"There's more. When Dana was beaten up, the cops arrested me and threw me in jail until Dana was able to tell them it wasn't me. Then I couldn't get the cops to put a guard on the room so a friend of mine and I are taking turns watching her. I was suspended from my job so I quit. I don't have any authority, in other words. When I find out when the shootings are supposed to happen, I'm going to try to get the Sheriff's Office to go out, but I see problems with no proof or evidence and the owner of the Golden Eagle being accused."

"Jesus, what a tangled web, huh? What can I do to help?" Maes sounded excited, which was what Bailey needed.

"Rudy, do you want to come and help me? I want to catch these no-gut bastards in the act, and there's one in particular I want to get."

"I can't just leave, not knowing how long I'd be, but call me when you know when this is going to come down and I'll be there in less than an hour and a half."

"Rudy, you realize we wouldn't be there as cops, I'm out and you wouldn't be in your jurisdiction, different county, federal land and all that shit."

"Hey Bailey, we'll do it from a common law standpoint. The public demands it. Or something like that." Maes chuckled then said, "You've got my cell number. I'll have my car loaded and ready to go when you call. The only thing that will keep me away is if I'm at a crime scene. I'll try to get covered for nights. Call me."

"Okay, Rudy. And thanks, I'll never forget this."

Bailey tried calling Hampston but was told he was unavailable. He called the cell number Mike had given him and was answered by a terse, "Agent Hampston."

"Mike, this is Bailey, can you talk?"

"Not now, Bailey. I'll call you later."

Bailey hung the phone up. Deciding to get some sleep, he fed the dog and went to bed after locking the house up.

Chapter Twenty-two

It was an hour after the sun had gone down, and with no moon, it was pitch-black. The wind was blowing gently out of the south as he sipped cognac, standing on his patio. Built on a large lot, his small, elegant house was hidden away from the other homes in the area. It was located near the back of the city park with huge pines and rows of poplar trees used as wind breaks. It was an isolated area in the heart of a neighborhood.

Gravel crunched. *It must be the deer, probably going to eat the rest of my flowers.* Sometimes a dozen or more would be feeding in his back yard.

A hand covered his mouth and pulled him back. He struggled and tried to cry out. His slippered feet made dull, soft thuds as they kicked against the wooden planks. He turned his head and their eyes met. The fear gave him a burst of strength, but the intruder was too strong. The knife slid under his ribs and up into his heart. He tried to pull the knife out but all he could do was slap at the hand holding the knife against him. Skin and handle touching. His life pulsed out of his chest with each beat of his wounded heart. Hands grabbed his shoulders and lowered him onto the patio, on his back.

His body was dragged into the house and put on the bed, then covered with a blanket. The intruder closed all the curtains in the bedroom then went to the desk and opened the drawers, picking papers out and looking at each sheet, then putting them back in the drawers. Satisfied after taking one last look around, he grabbed the bottle of cognac, locked the back door and left the house, taking the same trail through the trees he'd come down.

Chapter Twenty-three

Streck drove past the West Side Motel, one block up from the Sunset and cruised the parking lot. He saw the Pontiac parked in front of the end room. He pulled down a side street and parked behind the motel, then walked to the room and knocked on the door.

The curtain opened and Lynch peeked out. Seeing Streck he unlocked the door and opened it, standing to the side as he walked in. Gomez was lying on the bed.

"Gomez, I got a little job for you I think you'll like." He looked a number up in the telephone book then dialed it. "May I have Mrs. Calhoun's room, please? Oh, can I call in the morning? Okay, thank you." Streck hung the phone up and turned to Gomez. "I beat the piss out of Calhoun's old lady Saturday night. She's been in the hospital and she's still there. The switchboard wouldn't connect me to her room, but they said she would be there in the morning. Calhoun has a friend helping him. When I find out they're leaving the hospital, I want you there to fuck them up."

Gomez began to grin. In prison he would wait in the dark hallways of the cellblocks and beat the crap out of new prisoners as they were going to their cells. He only did it when they were by themselves. A few times he had used a shank when the new fish put up too good of a fight. It gave him a rush.

"Finally, some action. I think we need some money now, my friend." Gomez's smile dropped and his hand was by the pillow.

"That's what I was going to do. Here's $1500 each," Streck counted the money out in their outstretched hands. We gotta go back out to where we killed those horses and get them buried."

"Bury them! Are you shitting me?" Lynch was sputtering.

"Take it easy, Lynch. There's gonna be a backhoe out there and I'll dig some holes and scoop them in. I'll need you for mostly a lookout. I'm keeping low so I'm gonna crash here tonight."

Gomez looked at the beds. "There's only two beds, who's on the floor?"

"I'm taking one of them. You guys were cell mates, share the other one."

Streck pulled the cell phone out of his pocket and dialed a number.

"Hello."

"I need to know who the doctor is for Calhoun's old lady. There might be a special greeting when they leave the hospital. His personnel records should have it." He gave his cell number and hung up.

"You guys got anything to drink?" They shook their heads no. "Let's go get some. There's a liquor store down a couple of blocks."

The three got into the Pontiac, Streck in the back, and drove down to a drive-in liquor store. Streck ordered a 12-pack of Bud and a fifth of Old Crow.

"This work for you two?" He asked.

"I'd like to score a little dope to smoke," Lynch said over his shoulder.

"Wait until we're finished with the job," Streck warned, "then I'll buy ya some."

They drove back to the motel room and Streck flopped down on the bed with a glass of whiskey and a beer. Pulling a pillow up under his head, he said,

"Tomorrow night we're meeting that dumb-ass cowboy out at the canyon and we'll bury the horses. Then I'll get him to round some more up and put 'em in that small canyon we saw. Thursday night we'll go out and kill 'em, bury them and then we're done. I'll pay you guys off and you can split with the Pontiac. As a bonus. Sound okay to you?"

"Yeah." Both Gomez and Lynch said. Gomez pulled a chair out and took a blanket lying on the bottom of the bed Streck laid in and tossed it around his shoulders.

"When do I get to take out the woman?"

"Soon as I find out when she's leaving, you can go wait at the hospital and when they leave, do her. Hell, do them all." Streck upended the glass of whiskey then finished the beer.

Nine in the morning and the three of them were still asleep. Through the barrage of snoring, hacking and farting, the small chirp of the cell phone penetrated Streck's brain.

He flipped the cover open, "Yeah——all right——Rivers." Ending the call he rousted the others up. "Gomez, I'm hoping I'll know something in the next couple of hours."

    *   *   *   *   *   *   *   *   *

Jim called down to the reception desk at ten in the morning.

"Has Dr. Rivers said when Mrs. Calhoun can leave yet?"

"I'm sorry, sir, Dr. Rivers hasn't called in with any orders for Mrs. Calhoun."

Jim, never having been taught patience, called every fifteen minutes, with the answer being the same, though the girl at the desk was a little less courteous each time.

The receptionist was being overwhelmed by calls during that particular time. One of the calls was from Dr. Rivers, telling her to write down and tell the appropriate parties that Mrs. Calhoun could leave anytime after his 6:00 p.m. evening rounds that night.

A woman speaking broken English was trying to get directions to the rehab room, getting louder as the girl used elaborate hand gestures when the switchboard phone rang.

"Hospital, may I help you?"

Streck said in a low voice, "Can you tell me when Dr. Rivers will release Mrs. Calhoun?"

"I TOLD YOU, UP THE GODDAMN ELEVATOR, SECOND FLOOR! Oh my God, I'm so sorry sir. Just a minute...Mrs. Calhoun...after six tonight."

"Thank you so much." Streck could hear the phone ringing in the background as he hung up.

"She's leaving tonight, Gomez, after six. You take the car and find out where they're coming out. It'll either be a black Continental or a maroon Chevy extended cab pickup. When they bring her out, take them."

"You got a gun for me?"

"Come on, you're tougher than them. Use your knife."

Gomez grinned, his white chipped teeth flashing. Other than eating, they stayed around the motel room until Streck and Lynch left in the truck at 5:00 p.m. Gomez took the Pontiac and drove to the hospital taking the entrance to the back parking lot where he saw a black Lincoln parked.

Travis tried calling Bailey but couldn't get a hold of him. Williams hadn't come in that morning, missing a meeting with a corporate ranch manager interested in rotating grazing areas on leased land in conjunction with a government grant. With Calhoun suspended or having quit, Travis was the only one available to take the man out to the section of land being considered.

When he got back to town it was close to 6:00 p.m. He tried Bailey's home again and when no one answered, he called the hospital and asked for Dana's room.

"Hello." Jim answered the phone.

"This is Travis Knight, is Bailey there?"

"No, what do you need, something I can help you with?"

"I wanted to talk to him; maybe I'll come up to the hospital and see him there."

"You come up to the waiting room and call me, then when he shows up, I'll tell him you're there. Don't come to Dana's room. You got that?" Jim's voice had taken an edge on it; he still didn't trust the prick so he wasn't going to be too accommodating.

Travis drove up and parked in the front parking lot. He went to the reception desk and used the in-house phone to call Dana's room.

"Is Bailey there yet?"

"No, he should be soon. This important?"

"Not really, it might help him out, hell, maybe even you."

"Sit tight in the waiting room, and when he comes in, I'll tell him you're there." Jim hung the phone up and went outside the room as the nurses helped Dana get ready.

Bailey parked in the front of the hospital and came in through the visitor's doors and took the back elevator to the second floor. When he walked in Dana's room, Jim said, "That Travis guy is down in the waiting room in the lobby, wants to talk to you. He says it's not real important, but it might be something that could help me and you."

Bailey knew it didn't have anything to do with the horses, because that would have been important.

"Jim, why don't you take Dana down the back way and out to your car. I'll talk to Travis and meet you in the parking lot." He helped Dana and Jim get her things and rode with them down to the first floor. As they started towards the emergency room entrance, Bailey went to the waiting room in the lobby. When he walked in Travis was standing over by the window, looking out towards the front parking area.

Warily he approached, "What's up, Travis? What'd you want to talk about that'll give me and Jim some help?"

*　　*　　*　　*　　*　　*　　*　　*　　*

Jim and Dana slowly walked from the exit doors towards his Lincoln.

167

There was a stocky Mexican over by the ambulance wiping the side window. Something struck Jim as odd about a guy wiping a window so late, but he couldn't think of what it was. He bent down to open the door for Dana when she screamed.

"Jim, look out!"

He turned and crouched as a fist hit him in the ear. He staggered back into the car and saw the Mexican coming in fast. Jim slipped the blow and back-knuckled Gomez in the mouth! He swung an overhand left, hitting him in the cheek. Gomez grunted and fell back, Jim moved in with a flurry of lefts and rights to the face and some hard shots to the gut. Gomez went to one knee, his hands holding his stomach.

Jim came in to snap kick the Mexican in the face.

Dana was frantically trying to run to the entrance door and screaming for Bailey. Her side felt as if it would burst from the exertion. She threw the door open, "Bailey——Bailey! Oh God! Bailey!" she screamed running down the hallway. A nurse came out of the x-ray room and told her to calm down.

"Bailey, help Jim!" Dana screamed as loud as she could.

Bailey heard a commotion in the hallway and started towards the door to the lobby. "Come on, Travis." He heard Dana screaming. Bailey slammed the door open and raced toward the screams.

Jim came in low; *I'm going to smash this fucker's face in*, when Gomez thrust up with his knife, putting his shoulder into it.

It felt like he had been hit with a fist, the knife was all the way into his stomach, just the handle sticking out. He felt an electric shock run up his chest; his legs went numb and as he saw the knife being pulled out by Gomez, he fell to the ground and rolled on his back. Gomez straddled him, holding Jim's hair in one hand and the knife in other. "Adios, mother fucker." Gomez said and raised the knife.

Bailey burst through the door running as fast as he could.

"HEY!"

Gomez saw him coming, jumped to his feet and swung the knife. Bailey countered the knife with a stiff forearm, then hit Gomez in the throat with a fist that had started from his hip. The splat of muscle and bone sounded like a side of beef being hit with a hammer.

Gomez's eyes bugged out, his hands went to his throat and he started gagging. The whistle of air being sucked in was strained and high pitched. He fell to the ground kicking. A nurse ran out and kneeled down by Gomez, checking his airway.

"He's about dead, this guy's hurt bad," Bailey said, pointing to Jim. "Get a gurney and get him into the emergency room." Bailey sounded calm and he went over to Jim and looked in his eyes. Blood was oozing out of the front of Jim's shirt. Bailey couldn't see Jim's chest rise, and his eyes were glassy slits.

"He's dead now." The nurse muttered. She got up and went over to Jim, feeling for a pulse.

"You better be alive or I'm going kick the crap out of you." Bailey spoke quietly, cradling Jim's head.

An eye opened. "Did I whip his ass?" His voice was very soft; it was taking an effort for him to speak.

"You betcha. You got his ass good." As much trouble as Jim was having breathing, Bailey wondered if the knife had gone into a lung.

"Come on you guys, hurry it up before we lose him!"

Two orderlies jogged up with a gurney, dropped the wheels and gently lifted Jim onto it. They raised it up and started wheeling it to the emergency room doors.

A doctor had come out and was checking his vitals. "Does anyone know how long of a blade?" He was compressing the wound to staunch the flow of blood.

"About an eight-inch blade, Doc." Bailey said after looking at the knife, still in Gomez's hand. He could hear a siren coming closer, he knew the cops would be here soon.

"Take him to surgery." The doctor ordered. "We'll have to evaluate after we go in."

Dana was standing by the doors, tears streaming down her face, shaking uncontrollably. Bailey went over and put his arms around her.

"He's going to okay. He's too damn mean to die. You're going to be all right, Dana. You're tough too. The cops are probably going to take me in until they find out it was self-defense. I need somewhere you can go. And not Jenny's. She can't protect you."

He pulled his cell phone out as the cops arrived. They had their guns drawn when they jumped out of the patrol car.

"Nobody move. Just hold it right there!" The first cop said. The gun swung from side to side, as if he didn't know who to cover. When he saw Bailey, the gun slid back into his holster.

Dana went over to the policemen. "My friend was attacked and knifed by that guy on the ground. He stabbed Jim and was ready to stab him again when Bailey got him."

The cop looked at Bailey. "Let me get this straight. The three of you were walking out and this guy jumped you with a knife?"

"No." Dana sounded exasperated. "Jim McConroy, our friend who was knifed, was escorting me to his car; Bailey was inside talking to Travis Knight. There, there's Travis. This guy came at Jim, and knifed him as they were fighting." Her eyes were tearing, she took as deep of a breath as she could and continued.

"He and Jim were fighting. I'd gone into the hospital and yelled for Bailey, who was talking to Travis in the lobby. When we got out, this guy had knifed Jim and was getting ready to stab him again when Bailey slugged him." She started breathing hard. "I can't move fast with this cracked rib."

One of the cops had radioed for the coroner. An orderly was laying a blanket over Gomez's body. "Don't disturb anything," one of the cops yelled.

"I'm not, just covering him up. Too many people looking out the windows. You don't want them to be looking at this, do you?" The orderly replied.

"No, that's fine." The cop said.

Two deputies from the Sheriff's Office showed up and told the cops they would work the crime scene if the cops wanted to take Bailey and Dana down to the police department. The cops put them in the back of the patrol car and asked Travis if he would follow them down and give a statement.

On the way to the police department one of the policemen called the dispatcher and asked if they would have the City Attorney meet them at the P.D. The City Attorney pulled in the same time as the police car.

"Mr. Calhoun, we seem to be dealing with you quite often lately."

The mayor had appointed Ralph Franklin. It wasn't like he had been the best choice; no one else wanted the job.

He was a pompous, self-important little man, impressed with himself and his office.

Franklin said, "Come on, get them all downstairs and we'll see what the hell is going on."

After they were gathered and sitting down in the PD's conference room, Franklin turned a tape recorder on.

"Okay, Ms. Calhoun, why don't you tell me what happened."

Dana looked at him, a fire beginning to light in her eyes.

"First of all, Mr. Franklin, it's Mrs. Calhoun and I'll expect you to address me in that manner for the remainder of this interview. Are we clear on that?"

Franklin acknowledged with a slight shake of his head, a blush creeping up his neck. Clearing his throat he said,

"All right. Now, *Mrs*. Calhoun, can you tell me what happened? And I would appreciate everyone waiting until she's done before speaking. I want a semblance of order while we do this. Please begin, Mrs. Calhoun."

"I had been attacked and beaten up Saturday night and was being released from the hospital tonight. The police wouldn't put a guard on the room, even though the man had threatened to get me again, so my husband called a friend, Jim McConroy, to come and give him a hand to protect me. His friend flew down from L.A. Monday morning and was escorting me out of the hospital when a stocky Hispanic attacked him. I ran back into———"

171

"Excuse me," Franklin interrupted, "Is McConroy the one who raised all the hell over Calhoun at the jail Monday?"

"Probably, no one let Bailey out of jail after I told the police he wasn't the one who beat me up. Anyway, I ran into the hospital screaming for Bailey. I couldn't run very fast or yell very loud because I have a cracked rib. Bailey heard me and ran outside where the Hispanic had knifed Jim and was getting ready to stab him again. He swung the knife at Bailey. Bailey slugged him and the guy fell down. I hadn't been that far in the hospital corridor so I was able to go back and see what had happened. Apparently one of the nurses or orderlies heard me screaming and called 911. The police came and here we are." She stared at Franklin, seeing if he was going to challenge her statement.

"Mr. Knight, what can you tell me?"

"Bailey and I were talking in the lobby waiting room when we could hear something going on. I couldn't distinguish any words but it was loud and panicky. Bailey walked out into the lobby then took off running. When I got in the lobby I could hear Dana screaming, so I ran to the parking lot to see what was going on. I saw the guy swing the knife at Bailey and then he was down on the ground. That's about it."

"Mr. Calhoun, can you add anything to this? Do you know who this person is, I mean was?"

"No, I'm investigating a BLM case and it could have something to do with that."

"You mean to say someone might be trying to get you so you won't prosecute them for stealing arrowheads or having too many cows on public land?" Franklin said. "I can hardly believe that scenario."

"I think you're right, Franklin. No, I don't know why this guy wanted to screw with us." Bailey was tired, and he wanted to get back to the hospital and see how Jim was doing.

Franklin stood up, "I'll have these statements typed up and if you will come in tomorrow afternoon, you can sign them. You all will have to attend the coroner's inquest later. My office will notify you when it's scheduled." He waited until everyone left then took the tape and put it in his briefcase.

As he was walking out he said to the policemen,

"Good work, men. So far it looks like it was justified."

Travis drove Bailey and Dana to the hospital.

"Bailey, I was up there to tell you I would be glad to give you guys a hand keeping an eye out on Dana. I can give you a break." He drew in a deep breath. "I don't know where Dad is now. He took Mom's Land Rover. If I can find him, I might be able to get the time out of him."

"Travis, I appreciate your offer. I've got an idea for Dana. The best thing you can do for me now is try to find your Dad or find out when they're going to kill those horses."

Dana had gotten out of the truck; Bailey closed the door and went up to the surgery waiting room. Dana was already there.

"He's in recovery, Bailey. The doctor said the knife perforated his liver and lung. His lung collapsed. It's going to be close. We need to call Linda."

"I'll call her, but first I need to get you somewhere safe. In fact I know who might help." He reached over for the phone and dialed a number.

"Dennis, this is Bailey, I need to ask you a favor." He held his hand up to Dana, who was starting to protest.

"Bailey, my God, when I heard about Dana, I couldn't imagine it. I've tried calling you to see how badly she was injured. Is she all right?"

"She's got a broken nose and cracked rib, plus her arm has some stretched ligaments. Dennis, I need to put her somewhere safe; someone tried getting her again tonight."

"Good heavens, Bailey, she can come and stay at my house. There's plenty of room and she'll have her own bedroom and bathroom. I might be a little slower on my feet right now, but I have a weapon. You and Dana can rest assured, she'll be safe here with me."

"Dennis, I'm going to be in your debt forever. I'll be out in a little bit. Leave your porch light off." He turned to Dana. "No argument, you're going to stay at Dennis's."

Bailey told the night nurse he would be back to check up on Jim, and then he went to his truck leaving Dana inside the emergency room. He opened the door and pulled his .45 out from under the shift console. Making sure a round was in the chamber, he put the gun in its holster and slid it on his belt. He started his truck and drove it around to the back parking lot and next to the exit doors. He walked back to the emergency room and putting his arm through Dana's, walked to the doors.

"I'm going to put you in the truck then I'll get in. Lock the door when you're in, then unlock it when I get to my door." He pulled his pistol out and kept it down the length of his leg. He opened the door and checked the small seating area in the back, and then put Dana in the front seat. She locked the door and Bailey came around the front.

Hearing the door unlock, he got in and put the truck in gear. He didn't see anyone around when he pulled out. Instead of turning east to head towards Dennis's house he turned to the west and accelerated out of town on a two-lane road. He fishtailed around a 90-degree corner, pulled to the side and shut his lights off. He held his gun up, ready to meet whoever might be following them, if there was someone. They waited in the darkness, not speaking. After a few minutes, Bailey turned his lights on and they drove back to Rawlins.

He took side streets and was eventually driving north on Third Street. Just before it turned into Highway 287, he exited onto the Sunset Hills Subdivision. The homes were new, nice and priced rather high, costing more than Bailey could afford unless he and Dana had been willing to make outlandish payments. The street made a serpentine route up to a two-house cul-de-sac. One of the homes belonging to Dennis. The porch light was off and the curtains were drawn.

Bailey parked in the front and turned off his lights. He let his eyes get accustomed to the dark then closed one eye and got out of the truck. He again had his pistol at his side as he opened Dana's door and escorted her to Dennis's front door. Quietly knocking, the door was opened immediately.

"Bailey, Dana, come in, come in." Dennis closed the door as they came in and took Dana's coat.

"Let me show you your room, Dana." He took them down a hallway and turned the lights on in a large bedroom.

"The bathroom connects through the door over there," pointing to a door on the other side of the room.

"Dennis, this is very nice. I hope I won't be an inconvenience staying here for a day or so." Dana smiled at him.

"Certainly not, your company will be enjoyed." He led them back to the living room and asked Bailey and Dana if they would like something to drink.

"None for me Dennis. I'm going back to the hospital to check up on my friend." Bailey looked at Dana. "Are you going to be all right?"

"Yes, call me when you can, and don't worry, I'm sure Dennis will take good care of me."

"Rest assured, Bailey, she'll be fine. I see an opponent for scrabble later." He held the door open after turning the lights low and carefully looking outside.

"Bailey, why did you close one eye when you were getting out of the truck?" Dana asked.

"An old FBI trick. The eye that's closed will have night vision when you open it in the dark. I didn't want the truck interior lights to cut it down." He gave Dana a kiss and hug then with his gun hanging by his side, he went to his truck and left.

"Dana, I want you to make yourself at home. I believe the saying is, 'mi casa, es su casa' or something like that."

"Thank you Dennis, I feel better already."

*   *   *   *   *   *   *   *   *

Bailey drove home and parked down the street. He had a lot of telephoning to do with the remainder of the evening. He walked up to his house hearing Callie bark as he approached the front of the house. "Good girl, that's about the first time your barking hasn't pissed me off." He went through the fence gate and the dog and he went into the kitchen.

His first call was to the hospital to see if Jim was out of the recovery room.

"He'll be in another couple of hours, then we'll transfer him to a room. He's out of danger, but still considered in serious condition."

Saying he would be up in the morning after Jim was in his own room, he called Linda.

"Linda, this is Bailey. Don't get upset, but Jim was hurt tonight. He was stabbed."

She yelled into the phone, "What do you mean he was stabbed? How bad is he hurt, Bailey?"

"They had to perform some emergency surgery. I just got off the phone with the hospital and they took him off the critical list and are calling him serious. He's going to be all right, Linda. I'm sorry this happened."

"I'll take the first flight out. If I fly to Salt Lake, my sister can drive me to Rawlins." She spoke in a matter-of-fact tone, already having the trip organized in her mind.

"Tell Jim I'll come right to the hospital. If he's able to, we'll fly him home and put him in the hospital here."

Bailey gave his cell phone number to her and told her to call him when she got to the hospital.

He was getting Rudy Maes' number out of his notebook when the phone rang. Answering it with a wary hello he was surprised it was Dana.

"Bailey, I've been forgetting to tell you what I found out about the bill on the refuge."

"Yeah, every time I've thought about asking you, something has come up." He had a feeling she was going to reveal something very interesting.

"I looked up the bill Congress had passed for the refuge." Bed covers rustled. "The Congressman who had raised so much hell about passing it tacked an amendment on the bill. Basically, there's to be a count on the horses June 1st. If the population is less than forty percent of the original eighty horses, then the refuge will revert back to the status of public land open for recreation, grazing and *exploration of gas, oil and minerals.*"

"That's why the Golden Eagle had a lease proposal in last month. That son-of-a-bitch Knight will have a lease if the refuge goes back." Bailey was almost shouting with excitement.

"Damn, that's what I haven't been able to figure out. Why would anyone put a lease in when the refuge wouldn't allow it? Why kill so many horses? If the horse numbers are under the minimum, Knight has it dicked." Bailey felt his anger building.

"Goddamn him."

"And the Congressman who put the amendment on the bill was from Nevada." Dana added.

"Williams has got to be in it up to his neck. Knight and Williams. They must have hired this Streck to do the dirty work. Listen, you get some sleep. If Dennis wants to pamper you, let him. I'm going to go see what Williams has to say."

"Bailey, you be careful. Don't do anything where Williams could screw you or jeopardize your case. And most important, don't get hurt. I love you."

Bailey drove to Williams's house and parked two houses up. He had left the fuse out of the truck so the interior light didn't come on. He silently crept up to the front porch and looked in the windows. No light, nothing moved. He rang the doorbell. Nothing, no one answered. Easing to the side of the house he couldn't see anyone on the patio or the back of the house. *He's probably with Knight, hiding out.*

Chapter Twenty-four

Streck and Lynch met Fritz Meade at Three Forks. Meade fired the diesel tractor up and followed Streck to the refuge turnoff. He was only able to go about a half-mile before the road was too rough for the tractor-trailer. He blinked his lights at Streck, then got out and started unloading the backhoe. When Streck turned around, Meade had the hoe unchained and the ramp set.

The backhoe was idling.

Meade called to Streck. "You any good at driving one of these? I can do it, I'm just not real good."

Streck climbed in and backed it off the trailer, then with the lights on, started down the road. Meade hopped into the driver's side of the pickup and took off following.

"What ya think?" Meade asked Lynch.

"Ain't thinking nothing but get this shit over with and get the hell out."

"Not me." Fritz replied. "I want to be in on fucking the government as much as I can."

It took nearly an hour for the backhoe to get to the canyon, and once there, Streck started digging a long wide ditch by the bodies of ten horses.

"Damn, you gotcha a lot of them fuckin' horses." Meade yelled.

Streck pushed the horses into the ditch with the frontend loader; tearing, cutting and dismembering as he scraped them into the hole. Covering the ditch up, he pulled over to individual horses and dug a single ditch and pushed the horses in. Some had to have a dragline tied to them and pulled over to the makeshift graves. As the sun was rising there wasn't a dead horse to be seen in the canyon. If anyone walked in, the graves were evident, but flying over or looking from a distance, they wouldn't be seen.

"Meade, could you come in later and lay some hay down, make it blend in?"

"Yeah, I could do that. I'll get some of my wetbacks to come and finish it up."

"How about rounding up one last bunch of horses up and putting them in the little canyon over south? Streck asked.

Though Streck had run the backhoe for nearly eleven hours straight, he felt energy flow through his body.

Meade spread his legs and stared at Streck. "Yeah, I can do that, but I'm gonna tell ya, I want in on the killing. Anytime I can screw with the feds, I ain't gonna miss out."

Smiling, Streck said, "I think this time we could use you. We're going to meet at Lamont around 9:00 p.m. tomorrow night. If you can have the horses inside the canyon, we'll do it. By the way, Calvin Knight will be with us. He wants to get in on the action too."

"All right! Gonna have us a big party." Meade whooped.

The morning was cold and getting colder. The wind was blowing from the north and was picking up speed. A front was moving in.

"She's gonna be raining or snowing tonight." Meade predicted. He walked over to Streck's truck and got in the back.

"Take me back to the tractor and I'll go to the ranch and bring my men

180

out to finish up."

"If you can't get the horses rounded up, call me on my cell phone. If I don't hear from you, we'll see you tomorrow night." Streck said.

With a wave of his hand, Meade started the tractor. Leaving the trailer behind, he headed back to the highway.

Streck and Lynch turned toward Rawlins and drove at a steady 60 mph. They stopped at Grandma's Café.

"Let's get some breakfast, then we'll head to town."

Minnie was behind the counter, setting plates and silverware into a storage bin. She looked at them coming through the door and felt a small tingle go up her spine.

They sat at a table towards the back of the café, Streck facing the door.

"Coffee?" Minnie brought cups and a coffeepot over, filling their cups and leaving the pot. She was going to sneak out and call Bailey, then remembered his warning not to do anything where they would be suspicious.

Both men ordered a big breakfast of hot cakes, eggs and bacon. Minnie went to the kitchen and started fixing the meal. She kept glancing over her shoulder at them.

"What's your problem?" The big one said.

"Nothing, I just thought I seen you in here before, maybe last week."

"That's right, you did. We came in and bought some beer. We're doing some seismograph work out north and staying in Rawlins."

After they ate and left, Minnie got on her telephone and tried calling Bailey. When he didn't answer at his house she tried the BLM office and was told he would be gone for an undetermined amount of time. Puzzled by the answer she tried his cell number but a recording said the phone was off or out of range. She reminded herself to try in a couple of hours and if she couldn't get him, she'd call Travis Knight. Maybe he could find Bailey.

Streck and Lynch hadn't reached Willow Hill when they turned the radio on as the news was finishing.

"The dead man has been identified as Juan Gomez, recently paroled from the Colorado State Penitentiary. No motive has been determined and the case is still being investigated."

"Jesus Christ! Gomez is dead?" Lynch yelled. Pounding the dash with his fist he said, "I'm gonna kill me that fuckin' BLM pig." His teeth were clenched, and he almost spit out the words. "Gomez and me known each other for ten years. Probably the only friend I had. You didn't think they'd have killed him, did ya, Streck?"

"Shit, no. Gomez was tough. There must have been a couple of them who took him." Streck pulled the truck over to a dirt road turn off and made a u-turn. Accelerating onto the highway he was going north again.

"What ya doing?" Lynch muttered. He was sitting with his head down.

"Gonna stay at Three Forks until tomorrow night. They got some cabins in the back I seen last time we went by."

The truck pulled into the gas station at Three Forks. Streck went into the office and asked if they rented cabins.

"Sure do, forty bucks a day. Clean and a bathroom. No phone or TV though."

Streck paid him the money and got the key. They drove around the rear of the station and parked in back of the second cabin. "We'll crap out here tonight. We can get some sandwiches in the station."

Chapter Twenty-five

The coffee was on when the phone rang. Carl Toomes's cigarette voice rasped a hello. "Hey, Bailey. I just flew over the refuge on my way back from Casper and you won't believe what I seen."

"Tell me, Carl. I'm not in the mood for guessing games right now." Bailey paused. "No more dead horses, I hope."

"Yeah, I seen horses, but they're alive. Somebody's got them in the little box canyon where they use to trap them on the roundups. You know the one I mean? West of Lamont about six or seven miles."

Bailey could visualize the area in his mind and knew the location. "I know it. Did you see anyone around?"

"Nope, just the horses. There was a backhoe holding a gate or something blocking the entrance. But that was it."

"Thanks, Carl, you don't know how much this has helped me."

Bailey replaced the receiver and pulled a topographical map out of the desk drawer and turned to the Green Mountain section. He ran his finger over the page, stopping at the box canyon marker. *You guys might of just fucked up.*

The telephone rang again, bringing him back from his thoughts. Bailey picked it up and wasn't surprised that it was Linda.

"Bailey, I'm at the hospital. The doctor will be here around 9:00 a.m. and if Jim can take it, we'll charter a flight out this afternoon."

"I'll be up in fifteen minutes, Linda. Stay around people; I don't know what the hell could happen."

"I called the police and they have an officer here. He'll stay until we leave."

The power of a woman, Bailey thought. "Okay, I'll be up in a little bit."

He grabbed his cell phone and started to put it on his belt when he heard the quick beeps. "Son-of-a-bitch! The battery's low." He stuck it in the charger, fed the dog and left for the hospital.

As he drove up the street, papers and trash were skittering down the sidewalks. The wind had increased its force and was bringing dark clouds that marked snow or rain with it. *We're going to have a storm today or tonight.* He wondered how low the temperature would drop.

He pulled into the hospital and parked in the back parking lot. He saw the blood had been washed off the asphalt leaving a small trickle of water draining towards the storm drain. Looking around, he had his hand on his pistol and opened the door. After the events of the last night, he had half expected someone to run out at him, hoping a little that Streck would try to take him there, while he was ready. No one jumped out nor shot at him as he walked from the cover of car to car, then to the emergency room doors. He strode down the same hallway he had run through just hours ago, getting to his friend and Dana as fast as he could. Now, his friend was in the hospital and one man was dead.

This had turned into a deadly confrontation. Pushing the button in the elevator for the third floor he stood to the side when it opened. He could hear the nurses talking at their station around the corner and there was a janitor mopping down the hall. A city cop he vaguely knew was sitting in a chair outside the room. He recognized Bailey and nodded to him.

184

Linda came out of the room facing the station.

"If the doctor releases Jim, we'll be leaving by noon. I'll expect everything ready to go. Is that clear?"

"Yes, Mrs. McConroy." The nurse spoke in a subdued voice.

Bailey hesitated for a moment, and then as Linda started back into the room, he said, "Linda, how are you holding up?" He hugged her and kept his arm around her as they entered the room.

A raspy, hoarse, voice spoke, "For Christ's sake, Calhoun, you trying to hit on a near-dead man's wife?"

Linda patted Bailey's arm.

"See, he's a smart-ass already, he's ready to fly."

There was an IV in Jim's right arm and he was pale but sitting up. He was sucking down water through a straw and grimaced when he put the glass back.

"Dammit, Jim. The doctor told you not to stretch. Now, knock it off or I'll get Bailey to tie you to the bed."

"And I'll do it too, you big bastard!" Bailey laughed as Jim tried to act offended.

The doctor came in the room and greeted Linda and Bailey, "How's everything today?" He took his stethoscope and placed it on Jim's chest, then felt under his chin and opened his gown.

"How's the incision feel, Mr. McConroy? Other than tight and hurting, does it feel hot?" He placed his hands gently on the area around the wound.

"My chest and gut hurt like hell, Doc, but no, not hot."

"We gave you two units of plasma last night for the blood loss. I believe if he uses oxygen, Mrs. McConroy, we can let him fly by air ambulance today." Picking up the chart he scribbled something only God and nurses can read, then smiled and told them to call him if there were any problems.

"Have a safe journey," he said as he looked at his beeper going off and left the room.

Linda dialed a number and held Jim's hand as she spoke into the phone.

"Hello, this is Mrs. McConroy. The doctor has given the okay for Jim to fly as long as he has oxygen———fine. We'll be at the airport at 1:00. Bye." She hung the phone up and led Bailey out into the hallway.

"He was real lucky, Bailey." Tears formed in her eyes. "I don't know what I would do without him. He's such an ornery shit, but a lovable one. I know you have some important things going on, so tell him goodbye and then you'd better leave. We'll get out to the airport by the ambulance so there's really no reason for you to stay."

Bailey wasn't sure if he was getting a polite kiss-off or if she really wanted him to take care of his business. He hoped it wasn't the brush-off. If it was, nothing would ever be the same between Jim and Bailey. He went in the room and stood by the foot of the bed.

"Well, sport. You're going be heading out in a little bit, so I'm gonna say so long now. I don't know how to thank you, Jim and———"

"Jesus Christ, Bailey. You sound like a little wuss. Get out of here and call me when you get this shit done. Whoever's behind this needs to pay. You understand?"

"Yeah, I do. And they will." He patted Jim's leg and hugged Linda, then left the room. When he got out of the elevator he went to the receptionist desk.

"Hi, were you on yesterday?" He leaned on the counter and smiled.

"Yes I was, and what a day." She smiled back at him.

"It was my friend who was injured last night out in the back, and I'm trying to figure out how someone knew we would be leaving then. Dr. Rivers left a message with you to let me know when he was going to release Dana Calhoun, didn't he? I'm her husband."

"Yes and your friend had called about every fifteen minutes asking. Right after Dr. Rivers called I was having a problem with———oh no!" She turned pale and looked like she was going to cry.

"This woman was arguing with me and the phones were ringing off the hook. I remember now someone asked if Dr. Rivers was releasing Mrs.

186

Calhoun, and God, I thought it was your friend again. I told him around six; I'm so sorry, I was arguing with a woman who couldn't speak English very well." She put her hands over her eyes and softly started crying.

"It's all right. This would have happened anyway. It wasn't your fault."

He left through the emergency room doors in the back and went to his truck.

He parked at the curb outside the BLM office and rode the elevator to the second floor. Walking in, Dora stopped typing and looked at him, then said, "I don't think you're supposed to be here, Bailey."

"Where's Williams, Dora?" He glanced in the glass door of Williams's office but it was vacant. The desk was clear of any paper and no coat or hat on the hanger.

"He hasn't been in for a couple of days." She sniffed, "I haven't talked to him or seen him since Tuesday. Travis went to his house, but no one answered the door."

"Is Travis around?" Bailey could see he wasn't at his desk but who knew? Maybe he was in the can.

"He's at Roodmier's place. There was a complaint Roodmier was pumping water out of the river for irrigation."

"Will you give him a message for me? Tell him to call me if he has anything. Thanks, Dora." She was still sitting at her desk and wiped her eyes as he left.

Chapter Twenty-six

Streck woke up around noon the next morning, yawning and scratching his balls. He went and pissed, pulled his pants on and walked to the gas station. Opening the cooler, he pulled half a dozen sandwiches out and picked up a six-pack of Bud. He paid with a fifty-dollar bill and trotted back to the cabin. A storm front was moving in. The wind blew out of the north and he thought it would start raining or snowing any minute.

"Lynch, wake up. I've got some food and beer." He kicked the door shut and Lynch jumped up as the door banged shut.

"Dammit, Streck, quit fucking with me. I'm getting tired of it." He shouted.

"Hey, sure, sure. Don't get bent outta shape."

When Lynch got out of bed and came back from the bathroom, he said, "Soon as this is over, I'm getting out of here. I'm starting to get spooked; too many bad things happening." He picked up a sandwich and took a bite.

"What happens to Gomez's money?" Lynch asked.

Streck opened a beer and took a long swallow.

"I think we should split what he was gonna get. Unless you want to give it to his family."

"Fuck 'em. A split sounds good. 50/50, right?"

"You got it." Streck pulled the cell phone out of his pocket and poked a number. He was still for a moment, then with a frown he said, "Nine tonight. You better be there." He flipped the phone shut.

"Isn't that a little risky, leaving a message?" Lynch asked between bites.

"Yeah, but he's not answering or not there. He'll show."

*   *   *   *   *   *   *   *   *

Travis left Roodmier's with a face red from anger. He had seen the big pump sitting by the river, the gas motor screaming and the water spraying into a huge reservoir. He shut the motor down and was going to drive up to Roodmier's house when the back door banged open and Neal Roodmier came flying down the embankment.

"What the hell are you doing, Knight? Get off my property."

"You know you can't pump from the river, Roodmier. It's against the law." Travis got out of his truck and faced him.

"You start this pump back up, I'll hang your ass."

Roodmier's face had turned a bright crimson.

"You government people are always out to screw us little folk. Someday the tables will turn. And I hope I'm there."

"You just remember what I said. Don't start that pump again. You want to come in to apply for a pumping permit, then do it. But, goddammit, you do it legal." Travis got in his truck and without looking at Roodmier again, turned around and drove onto the road. He saw Roodmier flipping him off in the rear view mirror.

Asshole. He left Ft. Steele and headed west to Rawlins. What really burned him was the surrounding land was dry and littered with sagebrush. It needed to be irrigated. If Roodmier would get a permit, there wouldn't be a problem. The BLM wasn't unreasonable; they just wanted procedures followed.

When he got to Rawlins he turned at Sheep Hill and pulled into the driveway of his parent's house. Knocking on the back door, he went in when no one answered. He yelled for his mother, but there wasn't any response. *She must be out socializing*, he thought as he walked into the den. He noticed the light blinking on the answering machine of Calvin's private line, and looking around to see if his father was lying in wait for him, he pushed the play button.

"Nine tonight, you better be there." There was a click then the date and time were given in a computerized voice.

"Hell," he said out loud. "It's going down tonight." Travis hurried out of the house, and hopped in his truck, started it and drove to Bailey's home.

Bailey's truck wasn't in front of the garage and when he rang the doorbell, no one answered. The dog was barking from inside the fence. He got back into his truck and called the office.

"Dora, this is Travis, I won't be in the office this afternoon, I have some things I need to get done."

"All right. By the way, Bailey Calhoun was looking for you, Travis. He wanted you to call him if you found out anything."

*   *   *   *   *   *   *   *   *

When Bailey had left the office he called Dana on his cell phone while still parked at the curb in front of the BLM.

"How are you feeling?"

"Better, Bailey. Dennis has been great. Everything still hurts but not quite as much. Is Linda here yet?"

"Yeah, she got here and she's flying Jim back to L.A. In fact they're probably in the air now. I think she's really pissed." Bailey was surprised it was past noon already. Where the hell has the time gone? He thought.

"You can't really blame her. You had him come down to help and he ends up stabbed and in the hospital and you're, thank the Lord, not hurt." Dana said the last gently; she knew Bailey was feeling guilty.

"Dana, this should be over in a day or two, then we'll get our lives back

191

together. I know I sure as hell need to."

"You be careful, Bailey. Both of us won't be able to stay at Dennis's house. He'll have another heart attack if he tries taking care of both of us." A small laugh escaped from her. It sounded good to hear, Bailey thought.

"I'll try to keep you posted when things break. Is Dennis there now?"

"No, he went to the grocery store. Probably to get more ice cream and nuts. I can see why he had the by-pass. My goodness, he eats a lot of crap. But don't worry, I've got the door locked."

Bailey chuckled at her idea of Dennis's shopping list. "Remember, don't take any chances. I can't finish this if I have to worry about you being safe."

She started to protest, then told him not to worry; she would be fine.

He flipped the phone off. Pulling away from the curb he was struck by the feeling of weariness. Not remembering when he had slept for more than a couple of hours, he thought he'd go home and try to grab a quick hour of sleep. He plugged his cell phone into the charger and sat down in the re-cliner.

When he opened his eyes, it was dark outside. The wind was howling out of the north and rain pelted the windows. Bailey got up, surprised at how dark it was and went to his truck. He started down the street and had a diffi-cult time seeing out the windshield.

"Don't even take a deep breath." The barrel of the pistol pressed against the back of his neck. Streck's form rose up from the back and Bailey could smell the foul odor emanating from him.

"I've been waiting for this, Calhoun."

Bailey couldn't make out what he looked like; it was too dark in the back of the truck. Suddenly he floored the gas and the truck shot down the street.

The gunshot was deafening, reverberating throughout the cab. The pickup swerved to the left, then went into a slide coming up on two wheels, causing it to roll over and over down the street, doors flying open, bodies being thrown out.

The phone rang again. Bailey sat up with a start. *Jesus Christ, I haven't*

192

had a nightmare like that for years. He reached over and picked up the phone.

"Calhoun." He felt some sweat slide down his face.

"Bailey, it's Travis. You okay?"

"Yeah, Travis, I was just dozing and the phone woke me up. You got something?"

"Yeah, it's going to be tonight, Bailey. There was a message on Dad's private line. It said tonight at nine. It sounded like Streck."

"How do you know it's tonight? Maybe it going to happen tomorrow."

"The answering machine has a date and time stamp. The call was a little while ago."

"What are you gonna do, Travis? I'm going to get the Sheriff's Office to come out, but do you want to come, beings your Dad will be there?"

"I want to help, Bailey. No one has the right to do what my father has done or at least been involved with. What time?"

"Let me go to the S.O. and see what they want to do. Do you have a cell phone?" Travis gave him the number. "Good. I'll call you in an hour or two."

Bailey drove into the Sheriff's parking lot and rang the buzzer at the back door. The deputy on duty was Larry Kelly, someone who Bailey had known and worked with on several different occasions. When Kelly saw it was Bailey, he pushed the electric lock opener and stood up from his desk.

"Hey, Bailey. Long time no see. What's going on?" He went to the coffeepot and filled a cup, giving it to Bailey, then filled his own.

"I need some help, Larry. I have it on good authority that tonight several men are going to kill some wild horses out on the refuge. There's a couple of problems. I don't have any concrete evidence and Calvin Knight is involved."

"Calvin Knight! Are you nuts, Bailey? Tell me what you have." Kelly looked at Bailey, his eyes wide and a smirk on his face.

"Last weekend, I found a total of thirty-five horses shot and killed. There was a group of fifteen and a group of twenty. I dug some bullets out and they

193

matched with bullets that were recovered from the wild horses killed in the Red Desert a couple of weeks ago. Deputy Maes is investigating that incident."

"I know Rudy," Kelly interjected, "He's a good man."

"Yeah, that's what I thought about him. I've been learning Dennis Cummings's job because he's retiring after open heart surgery and Williams is putting me in the position that handles lease applications, among other things. I found an application for the Golden Eagle to lease areas in the refuge. That didn't make sense because it isn't allowed. Then Dana found out that an amendment had been added to the refuge bill reverting the land back if the horse population decreased a certain amount by June 1st of this year. If that happens, then the Golden Eagle will get its leases and be able to explore for gas and oil on the refuge.

"When Dana was leaving work Saturday night, someone beat her up and gave her a message to tell me to back off and drop the investigation or they'd get her again."

"That's right, I saw where an unidentified woman was assaulted and entered into the hospital. Christ, I didn't know it was Dana. The city cops handled that one or I'd have known."

"Yeah, well, the cops threw me in jail thinking I'd beaten the shit out of Dana and I didn't get out until she was able to tell them it wasn't me. That happened on Monday. I had a friend come to help me watch her because the cops wouldn't post a guard."

Bailey shook his head in disbelief. "Jesus Christ, this is sounding like a soap opera. We're taking Dana out of the hospital Tuesday night and my friend gets knifed by some ass-hole, and I'm sure you heard what happened to him." Bailey saw he had Kelly's full attention, and Kelly knew Bailey had been the one who killed Gomez.

"I know the name of the guy who beat up Dana and according to Travis Knight, he and Calvin are meeting at Lamont tonight at nine to go out and finish off the horses. I don't know who else is in it for sure, but other than the circumstantial evidence right now, that's all I've got. But I do know they're going to do it tonight. Can you help me, Larry?"

"Haven't you heard the news, Bailey? There's a commuter plane down somewhere in the Medicine Bow Peak area and everybody's out there looking for it. I don't know if I could take the two other guys in town out. I'm not saying I don't believe you, but Jesus, you've spun a pretty farfetched tale."

Bailey's eyes turned hard and he stared at Kelly.

"It's not a farfetched tale. And I haven't spun shit. You know me, Larry; I don't go around telling crap like this for kicks. Forget it." He started for the door.

"Hold on, Calhoun, I didn't say I wouldn't help, I just said it sounded far-fetched. I'll get the guys who're are still in town and when I get off at 8:00 p.m., we'll come out. If this doesn't play out, call the S.O. and have them radio me, so we won't waste a trip. The Sheriff will probably be pissed anyway but you got my curiosity up. We'll try to be there as close to 9:00 p.m. as we can." He went to the big wall safe and pulled a portable radio out and handed it to Bailey.

"This is on our channel; take it so we can be in contact."

"Thanks, Larry, I owe you big time." He took the radio and started for the door.

"Bailey, I heard you got suspended, that right?"

His hand stopped in mid-air by the door handle. He took a deep breath and faced Kelly.

"Yeah, but its bullshit. Williams says it's because I was thrown in jail for assault and domestic violence, but it's not true. Total bullshit."

Kelly nodded his agreement. "We all thought that too, Bailey."

When he crossed the lot to get to his truck, rain was spitting down intermittently. A big gust of wind rocked the Chevy. Bailey thought it would be one hell of night to be out at the refuge. While he was still sitting in the parking lot, he took his cell phone and called Rudy Maes's number.

"Maes," he answered on the second ring. "What can I do for you?"

"Rudy, this is Bailey Calhoun, in Rawlins."

"Bailey, what's going on? Got anything new?"

195

"Yeah, I got a hell of a lead. It's going to happen tonight, Rudy. They're going out and shoot some more horses. You want to come and get in on the action?"

"You bet your ass I do. I'll leave in a half an hour. Where do you want me to meet you at?" His footsteps walking down a hallway echoed through the phone.

"Just call me when you get to town. Listen, Rudy, lots of things are going on. There might only be three of us for a while and it's dangerous. A friend of mine has been stabbed because of this. If you don't want to do it, I'll understand."

"I want to do it; I'll just bring more fire power. Is your friend okay?"

"Yeah, he was damn lucky."

"Good. I'll see you in two hours." Maes said.

As Bailey drove onto the street, he dialed another number.

"Hello, Cummings's residence."

"Dennis, this is Bailey, can I speak to Dana?"

"Bailey, I'm sorry, she hasn't been feeling well today and she's asleep now, but I'll wake her if you like." He could hear the concern in Dennis's voice.

"No, that's okay. Let her sleep."

"What's going on, Bailey? Anything I can do to help?"

"I'll tell you later, just be sure Dana stays safe."

"You can count on me, Bailey. Godspeed."

The wind made the truck shake as Bailey drove to his house. He parked in the driveway and looked around before he got out. When he saw Callie standing against the fence pawing at him, he knew no one was around the house. He went in the front door then let the dog in the back and fed her. He called Travis and told him Rudy Maes was coming from Rock Springs.

"Travis, if you can be here in a couple of hours, we'll sit down with Rudy and decide what we're going to do. I found out where the horses are

196

being held; we've finally had some luck.

"I'll be there, Bailey. We'll work something out. Hey, man, thanks for trusting me." The phone clicked in Bailey's ear as Travis hung up.

Something gnawed in the recesses of Bailey's mind, but he couldn't quite put a finger on it. It was like a touch of a cobweb; you felt it, but it wasn't solid.

He took his .45 out of its holster and disassembled it. Getting the gun kit and putting it on the kitchen table, he liberally oiled the pistol down. He took a soft cloth from the kit and cleaned the oil from the barrel and firing mechanism. Getting a box of SuperVel hollow points out of the closet, he loaded the clip and jacked one into the chamber, then took the clip out and put another bullet in it. There was a spare clip he loaded and stuck in his front pocket. He had a total of 15 rounds available.

Leaving the pistol on the table his pulse quickened when he thought of meeting Streck. Bailey wasn't a murderer, but it wasn't going to take much for him to kill the bastard. He'd do it without a moment's hesitation. If the opportunity didn't come, he was definitely going to beat him within an inch of his life. Justice took precedence, fuck the law.

The dog was nervous from the wind and storm moving in. Even Bailey jerked his head up when a gust rattled the windows. I wonder if Williams will be out there, he thought as he went to the coat closet. He took a jacket out with a waterproof cape on it and put some leather gloves in the pocket. He plugged the radio Kelly had given him into an electric socket to make sure it had a full charge. He felt like a warrior, ready to go to battle.

He saw the headlights as Travis pulled into his driveway an hour later. Fighting the wind he rushed through the open door Bailey was holding for him.

"Jesus, Bailey. The wind's gotta be blowing 30 mph." He slapped his hat against the side of his coat to shake the water off it.

"It's still spitting rain. I don't know if this storm will help us or hurt us." Travis said.

"Travis, the Sheriff's Office won't be able to come out until it's too late. Almost all the deputies are searching for the plane that went down. Larry

197

Kelly told me he'd bring a couple of deputies and come out when he gets relieved, about 8:30 p.m., but I don't think his heart's in it. I told him Calvin's involved and it didn't seem like he believed me. If you don't want in on this, I won't hold it against you."

"I wouldn't believe you either if I hadn't heard those phone calls. Think, Bailey, if I came up and said I thought the Sheriff was involved in this but had no real proof, would you believe me?" Travis was looking at the gun on the table.

"Do you think you'll need to use the gun?"

Bailey walked over to the window and looked out through the side of the curtain. He could see some deer coming down from the hills on their way to the cemetery to graze.

"No, I wouldn't believe you, and yeah, there might be some shooting."

Bailey's telephone rang and he picked it up on the second ring. "Calhoun."

"I'm coming in on the west side of town, Bailey; tell me how to get to your house." Rudy Maes said in an excited tone.

Bailey gave him directions, picked his pistol up from the table and slipped out the back door after telling Travis, "I'm going to just have a quick look see, just to make sure nothing is out of the ordinary."

He stayed to the side of the door until his eyes adjusted to the dark. The night vision was enough to see where he was going. Slipping around to the side of the house he mentally checked off the vehicles on the street noting there weren't any recent arrivals. When Maes drove up, Bailey met him as he was getting out of his car.

"Christ, Bailey, you startled me." He reached to the side of the seat and brought out a small duffel bag. He smiled, "My wares."

Bailey knocked on the door and Travis opened it, holding his hand out to Maes.

"Travis Knight, good to meet you."

Maes shook his hand and gave Bailey a questioning look when Travis told him his last name.

198

"Its okay, Rudy. Travis knows Calvin will go to jail. We can trust him."

Travis closed the door then turned to the men and said, "If there's a problem, Rudy, let's get it out now. I don't want you worrying about me if I'm behind you. There's no love lost between my father and me. It's bullshit if he thinks he can get away with this for the sake of getting richer."

"No problem, Travis. I appreciate your being up front with this."

Maes opened his duffel bag and brought out a radio and small pump shotgun, laying them on the table. A box of .00 buck was placed by the shotgun. He took a .357 Smith and Wesson in a holster from the bag with a large flashlight and put them with the rest of his tools of trade.

"What's the plan, Bailey?" He picked up the gun kit and went over the shotgun with the cloth.

"We'll take two outfits, mine and Travis's. We have to make it out there ahead of them so we can be there when they show up. I don't want them shooting any horses, but I want enough evidence to hang their asses."

"How do you know where they're going to be, Bailey?" Rudy asked a second before Travis.

"Carl Toomes called me yesterday; said he was flying over the refuge and couldn't find the dead horses in the canyon. There were twenty horses in there when we checked it out before. He flew over the small box canyon, you know where I'm talking about, Travis, west of the stage stop. Has the rock outcroppings that form the steep sides, and a small entrance." Travis nodded in recognition.

"He saw a herd in the bowl with a backhoe blocking the entrance. He circled low to see if anyone was around but didn't see anything. He said it's the buckskin's herd. They aren't getting these horses." As he was finishing the story he was picking up his pistol and sliding the holster on his belt.

"You brought your gun, Travis?"

Travis pulled his coat aside and the Government Issue .38 was at his side. "I've brought some extra ammo, I'm ready."

"Rudy, you ride with Travis. We'll drop down Willow Hill and turn off on the old Uranium Mill road. Just follow me, Travis. We're taking some back roads that avoid Lamont, in case someone's there early."

Maes put his gun on and loaded the shotgun. Bailey took the radio Kelly had given him.

"Rudy, you got a S.O. radio?" Maes told him he did.

"That's what this is; put it on the 331 frequency and we can use them to talk to each other while we're driving."

They got into their outfits and pulled away, heading north into the teeth of the spring storm and the possibility of death for one or all of them.

The small caravan of two vehicles came down Willow Hill and turned west on the Uranium Mill road. It was dark from the storm, but the rain had quit. No other set of vehicle lights could be seen on the highway.

When they turned north on a rutted dirt road, Bailey's cell phone rang.

"Calhoun." He felt like he should yell into it as the static drowned out half of the voice.

"Bailey, this is Mike Hampston. You there?"

"Yeah, I can barely hear you, Mike." Bailey stopped and showed his phone to Travis and Maes when they pulled along side and looked questioningly at him through the side window.

"My man came through. The informant had some interesting shit to tell." Hampston was enjoying his dramatic buildup.

"Mike, quit bullshitting around, I'm gonna lose you before you tell me what the hell you got."

"Okay, okay. There's a connection from Las Vegas. You're not going to believe this."

Bailey ended the call and started off again. His emotions were running high already and now he felt as if his head would blow off. He made his decision and hoped to God that he made the right one. If he didn't, he knew he'd spend the rest of his time in hell.

It was tougher going at first. The dirt road was slippery, and they put both outfits in four-wheel drive. After they had traveled several miles down, the road was a little smoother and they were able to pick up some speed.

They came up to the south side of the bowl and pulled behind the backside of a sand dune. The rise of the dune with huge clumps of sagebrush on the top would keep them from being seen. There was a road ahead of them that came in from the east and traveled up the side of the canyon and ended at the crest of the sides forming the bowl.

The inside walls of the bowl were only about twenty feet tall with rock outcroppings actually forming the sides. The surrounding outside area of the bowl consisted of small shale rock, boulders and brush and sloped approximately seventy-five yards to the rocks and sagebrush below.

Bailey took a tarp out of his truck and carried it to the top of the dune.

He laid it over two large chunks of sagebrush forming a small shelter and anchored it down with rocks. Going over to Travis's Tahoe, he climbed in the back.

"There's no use all of us freezing our asses off waiting for them to show. We can take turns watching from under the tarp. I'll take the first watch. When they show, we'll wait until they get up to the top before we move in."

Bailey climbed up the dune and slid under the tarp, looking to the east, the direction he thought they would come.

"God, I hope I'm not making the biggest mistake of my life tonight." He whispered.

So much had happened in such a short time. He knew it would end tonight. One way or another.

    *   *   *   *   *   *   *   *   *

"What do you know about Bailey, Travis? You've worked with him for a couple of years, haven't you?" Maes leaned back in the seat and spoke in a voice that had interrogated many people over the years.

"I hate to say this, Rudy, but not much. I thought he was one of the old guys that ought to retire. I wanted his job. But even with me pissing him off most of the time, he's treated me fair. I hope I get a chance to know him better. I'd like to have his respect." He said it with longing. Travis opened his window, looked up to the sky and took a deep breath.

"What little I've had to do with Bailey," Maes told him, "I think the guy has principle. As the cowboys used to say, 'He's one to ride the river with.' Travis, I want to get this out in the open. I'm asking because I don't want to worry about you not covering my back. Your old man being in it. I need to know you'll be with us from the start, no matter what happens. I know you already told me once, but I need to hear it again."

"I'm not sure how I feel about my Dad being involved. Pissed, but I half feel sorry for him doing something like this for money. But don't worry, Rudy, he doesn't deserve any special treatment. I won't let you or Bailey down, I swear it." He looked at Maes with an intensity that buried any of Maes' doubts.

*   *   *   *   *   *   *   *   *

Headlights. Coming from the east, like he figured. The reflection against the clouds spread out enough for him to decide there were at least two out-fits. How many men? They were about a mile away and would be to the bowl in minutes. Bailey's hand checked the holster's thumb break on the .45's hammer.

Chapter Twenty-seven

Streck looked out the curtains through the dirty windows and saw the storm still picking up force. He went out to the truck and brought some heavy coats back with him, throwing one to Lynch. Under his coat he had the rifles, including the one Gomez had used.

"We need to oil these down in case it rains on us." He had some rags and gun oil he put on the small table with the rifles. Sitting down, he started to rub the oil on the weapon in a loving, almost erotic manner.

"There's nothing like a fine rifle, Lynch. Keep her in good shape and she'll never let you down. Here——." He threw the oily rag to Lynch.

Lynch never gave a big shit about maintenance, whether it was a car or anything else he used, so he slid the rag over the barrel and dropped it in the corner.

"When are we going?" Lynch looked like he was pouting as he got up from the bed.

"Here in a little while. If Knight doesn't show, you, me and Meade will finish the job, then I'll make Knight a believer in keeping his appointments."

203

Streck pulled some money out his pocket and gave it to Lynch.

"Go get us some food over at the station. Get a six-pack too."

*   *   *   *   *   *   *   *   *

Grabbing the money and shoving it in the pocket of his jeans, Lynch jogged over to the station and fought the wind to pull the door open.

"Fuckin' wind, does it ever quit?"

The owner of the station came around the counter.

"Watch your mouth, I don't go for talk like that around my wife."

Lynch crouched a little. "Get out of my face. You don't like what I say, then too bad, do something about it." He smiled, showing his broken yellow teeth.

"Shouldn't talk that way around women, that's all." The man stepped back behind the counter. He was a fairly big man and bristled, but didn't say anymore. His wife was busy wiping a window. She didn't look up, just kept wiping.

Lynch picked up beer, sandwiches and chips and tossed them on the counter.

"How much?" He pulled some bills out of his pocket and picked a $20 bill out and dropped it by the food. "This ought to take care of it."

"Fourteen dollars even."

"Keep the change." He smiled, knowing the money was Streck's.

Lynch took a plastic sack from the counter top and put the food and chips in it, then picking up the six-pack he opened the door and let the wind slam it against the wall. He didn't close it after he left.

"The goddamn son-of-a-bitch, who'd he think he was, talking to me like that? I'm a veteran." The proprietor shoved the door closed.

"Watch your mouth, Homer, the Lord's listening; don't use his name in vain."

"Oh, shut the fuck up, Mildred." He went out the back door to their house trailer, slamming the door as he left.

*   *   *   *   *   *   *   *   *

Lynch pulled the door shut behind him as he pitched the sack of food to Streck. He opened a beer and took a long, greedy swallow. Streck had put the food on the table and was looking at the sandwiches as he pushed the beer tab open.

"Where's my change?"

"I let them keep it. Wasn't much and they seemed like such nice folks."

Streck knew Lynch was lying to him, maybe trying to get one up on him; he'd wait until after tonight's work, then he'd straighten his ass out.

After they had eaten and packed their things into the truck, Streck told Lynch to keep his rifle up front.

"We're at the point that if a cop stops us, he'll be dead meat." Lynch just nodded and put the rifle in the seat between them.

They saw Meade's truck parked across the highway from Grandma's Café and pulled in next to him.

Meade rolled his window down and asked Streck where Calvin was.

Streck looked at his watch. "We'll give him fifteen more minutes then go do the job by ourselves."

Meade held a thumb up, then lit a cigar and turned on his radio.

*   *   *   *   *   *   *   *   *

Calvin had called his private phone number at home and listened to his messages after he punched in the code. Hearing Streck's message, he sighed, locked up his cabin and headed toward Rawlins and then Lamont.

He saw the two trucks parked off the highway and pulled in next to them. Streck got out of his truck and came over to the passenger side of the Land Rover, motioning for Calvin to unlock the door. Opening it, he sat down and looked the SUV over appreciatively.

"Nice outfit, Calvin. The money must pour in to you, huh?" Streck grinned knowing Knight didn't like to be around him.

"I think my girl friend, Patsy Mae, might like something like this. She always liked nice things." He let go a laugh that made Knight jump in his seat.

"Pull next to Meade and we'll get going."

Knight started the Land Rover and backing up, turned and pulled up by Meade's truck. Streck powered his window down and leaned his head out the window.

"Meade, get in with Lynch and we'll follow you. When we get up on top we'll try to shine the lights on the horses. I'm gonna give you and Calvin here first shot."

"Sounds good to me." Meade got out of his truck carrying a bolt-action rifle and climbed in with Lynch.

"Go up here about fifty yards then go through the first gate you come to. We got about six miles going in this way."

"Why don't you drive? I don't drive trucks good, especially if the roads are shitty." Lynch put the brake on, and slid over when Meade walked around the truck getting into the driver's side.

"I don't care what Streck says, Lynch, you're half-smart."

Lynch didn't think Meade was funny, but he'd wait, maybe shoot the smart-mouth fucking rancher in the back when they finished with the horses. *Yeah, that's what I'll do. I'll just walk up and let him have it. Once in the back of the head.*

They drove north about 50 yards and Meade turned onto a dirt road heading west after driving through an open gate. Calvin and Streck followed in the Land Rover.

* * * * * * * * *

Minnie had seen the two trucks sitting together across the highway. After a bit she looked out the window as a Blazer-type outfit pulled up.

There were only two tables with people eating and they weren't calling for her so she told them to holler if they needed anything, then slipped out the door and stood in the dark, facing the trucks across the road from her.

When they drove up and turned through the BLM gate and headed west she went back in and dialed Bailey's cell phone.

"The cell phone you are trying to reach is either off or in a non-service-able area." The recorded voice said.

"Damn, where the hell is he?" She looked up Travis's home number and heard the ringing until she disconnected. She dialed one more number.

"Carbon County Sheriff's Office, Deputy Kelly speaking."

"Larry, this is Minnie at Grandma's Café."

"Hi, Minnie, what can I do for you?"

"Bailey Calhoun had talked to me a couple of days ago about watching for anything suspicious around here. I seen three outfits across the highway huddled together, and two of them just left and are headed west on the back road to Green Mountain. That's the road that goes to the horse refuge too. I've tried calling Bailey and Travis Knight, but I can't get nobody."

"Do you know what kind of outfits, Minnie?"

"No, they left a pickup and they're in a truck and Blazer looking thing now. I'm kinda worried, Larry."

"Minnie, if they're gone, can you run across the highway and get the license number off the outfit they left?"

"Yeah, but it'll take me a couple of minutes. I'm going to put the phone down, but you stay on, okay?"

"I'll be right here, Minnie. Be sure to write it down so you don't make a mistake on the number."

Minnie grabbed her ticket book and a flashlight then rushed across the highway as fast as she could. Shining the light on the truck's license plate, she wrote the numbers down then checked it again. Satisfied they were right, she half-trotted back to the café.

"Minnie, what are you doing? You look like you're gonna fall on your face." A voice from one of the tables said. The man was a local patron and had never seen Minnie go so far, so fast.

Panting, she picked the phone back up, "Wait a minute while I catch my breath." She held the phone next to her breast and poured herself a glass of water. After taking two swallows she spoke back into the phone.

"Here's the number, Larry." She read it off, then repeated it. "What should I do?"

"Hold on, let me run this through the computer." A moment later, "For Christ's sake, sorry Minnie, this is listed to Fritz Meade. That'd be about right. Don't do anything other than keep an eye out to see if those outfits come back. Most of our guys are gone, but I'll find some people and head out there. Call the office and have them relay anything to me over the radio if something else comes up."

"All right. I think you need to hurry." Minnie put the phone down and went over to the sign in the window turning it to say "Closed." When the last diner paid and left, she shut the lights off in the dining room and sat near one of the front windows and looked to the west.

Chapter Twenty-eight

When Bailey saw the lights, he went down to the Tahoe and told Travis and Maes. The three men climbed up the dune and sat under the tarp watching the approaching vehicles.

The truck downshifted and slowly climbed up the side of the bowl to the top, followed by the Land Rover. They swung toward the north and parked with their headlights still on. The Rover was behind the truck and to the side.

"Shit, that's Mom's Land Rover," Travis hissed through his teeth.

"Let's go. We've got to get up to the top from this side. It's gonna be rough and slippery from the rain, so be quiet and careful." Bailey motioned for Maes to follow him as he started up the side. Travis brought up the rear.

As they climbed up, their feet would slip out from under them from the treacherous footing. Fortunately, with a head wind blowing so hard, the sound was carried away.

Maes stumbled to his knees, then slid down into a rock, hard.

"Oh, shit! Bailey!" He half yelled.

Bailey came down to him. "What happened?"

"I fell and cracked my knee on this goddamn rock. I think I might of broke it." He tried to get to his feet and dropped back down. "Goddammit, I can't stand up, Bailey. Help me."

"If we have to carry you, you'll be more harm than help. Stay here and make sure none of them come down this way."

Maes started to protest.

"We don't have time to argue, and I don't know that we could get you up there anyway. See if you can get the Sheriff's Office on the radio, but keep it low." He turned and motioned to Travis, then started scrambling up the side.

When Bailey and Travis were near the top, they could see three figures in front of the Rover. Bailey pointed to the far side of the Land Rover and motioned Travis to go in that direction.

He pulled his .45 and held it down by his leg. He didn't want anyone to see a gun was in his hand. Crouching down he inched by the side of the Rover. He heard a soft thud and a sigh from the other side of it.

From behind him he heard, "Don't even blink."

Streck was standing behind him with an AR-15 pointing at his back. He had come from behind the Land Rover.

"You must be Calhoun. Not nearly as sharp as I figured." Streck kept the rifle pointed at him as he walked around Bailey, getting in front of him.

Meade saw Streck and tapped the other two men on their shoulders. "Hey, looks like you got one of them government pricks."

Bailey had turned a little to the side.

"What'd you do with Travis? Kill him?"

"Not yet, but I'm gonna. Then after I kill you, I'm gonna go see your old lady again. But I'm gonna fuck her before I kill her, you get my drift, Calhoun?"

*   *   *   *   *   *   *   *   *

In the bowl below, the horses were uneasy from the storm, the confinement and the lights. The buckskin came up to the brush fence partially held in place by the backhoe and shoved against it. He trotted around the herd, then moved to the inside, keeping them bunched. All the horses were jittery and on the move from the fear they felt.

*   *   *   *   *   *   *   *   *

Meade started walking towards Streck and Bailey, pulling the bolt back on his rifle and jacketing in a shell. He had a mean grin on his face.

"I've always wanted to kill one of you BLM assholes. Always telling us what we can do. You're gonna end up being fertilizer, Calhoun."

The shotgun boomed the same time Meade's body flew into the air. Streck crouched and cut loose with three shots into the darkness. Bailey pulled the .45 up and fired at Streck's chest. Streck was flung back from the force of the bullet. Bailey felt a burning sensation along the side of his cheek and dropped to the ground. Lynch was coming up, trying to unjam his rifle after grazing Bailey.

Two shots rang out from over the hood of the Land Rover, one hitting Lynch in the chest, the other putting a neat hole in his forehead. Travis, with blood dripping from his head, was still pointing his pistol at Lynch, then turned it towards his father, standing in the glare of the headlights.

Streck rolled over on to his side, and then stood up, holding one arm out; blood was on his jacket by his shoulder and the arm hung to his side.

"Fuck you, Calhoun." He smiled. "I could of whipped your ass pretty easy. 'Bout as easy as I beat the shit out of your old lady when I broke her arm."

Bailey hit him in the mouth, knocking him to the ground. Streck was on his hands and knees when Bailey kicked him in the side, rolling him towards the edge of the rocks. Every time Streck would get to his knees, Bailey would kick him in the side or chest. Bailey stood back as Streck hunched over.

Streck stood up holding the hunting knife. "Eat this." He thrust the knife towards Bailey. Sidestepping, Bailey slapped the knife away from him and hit Streck in the side of the head with the heel of his hand. Streck was knocked back and his feet started slipping on the edge of the rock outcropping. His arms pinwheeling, he fell off the side, striking rocks and landing at the feet of the stallion. The buckskin reared and came down on Streck with its front hooves. Streck tried crawling away with one hand in a weak attempt to pull himself away from the buckskin. Again the front legs battered the man lying on the ground; his life seeping out as the hooves tore into his face and chest.

The horses suddenly started stampeding. Streck's body tumbled and bones broke as the horses ran over it. The gate crashed apart from the sheer force of thousands of pounds of running horses slamming into it. At a dead run, they headed toward the north, the stallion leading.

Calvin stood with the look of a deer just before being hit by a car. His hand slid into his coat pocket and brought out a war relic Luger pistol.

Bailey had dropped his gun when he started fighting with Streck and he was too far from Knight to get him before he fired.

"Dad!" Travis yelled. "Put it down."

Calvin squinted into the headlights then put his hand over his eyes to shield them.

"Why? Why go this far for a stinking lease?" Travis sobbed.

"For you and your mother."

"Bullshit! You never cared."

Calvin looked to be contemplating his next answer.

"You're right, Travis. I never cared. It was for the money and power."

He stuck the pistol to his temple and pulled the trigger. His head rocked sideways and he dropped to the ground. His body twitched as the blood ran over his face.

"Damn you, why didn't you face it like a man? That's what you always told me." Travis covered his face with his hands.

Bailey found Maes lying on his side behind the Land Rover, his shotgun by his side. He had blood on his hip and was trying to sit up.

"They got me in the same leg that I broke." He grunted with pain. "I'm not bleeding too bad so they didn't get an artery. They all dead?"

"Three of them are. I've got to go down and check Streck; he fell over the edge and he's down on the bottom." A reflection of light caused Bailey to turn his head and look to the east.

"Here comes the Sheriff's Office." He could see red lights flashing in the distance. He picked up Maes's radio and called Kelly.

"Larry, this is Calhoun, can you read me?" The radio cracked with static.

"Bailey, we can see some lights west of us. Are you guys okay?"

"Rudy Maes was shot in the leg. I think it's broken; though he's not bleeding too bad. There's at least three dead, maybe four, but none of us."

"Hold on, Bailey, we'll be there in fifteen minutes."

Bailey gave the radio to Maes. "Rudy, stay in contact with them. I'm going to check Streck, then I've got some unfinished business in town. It won't wait."

Travis was by his father, looking down at the body. Bailey patted him on the shoulder and said, "Are you going to be all right?" Travis nodded.

"The S.O. will be here in a couple of minutes. I'm sorry, Travis, for your dad; for not trusting you." He slipped over the side of the outcrop and worked his way down to Streck.

Bailey couldn't recognize Streck's face, it just a mass of blood and broken bone. The body had taken a terrible pounding from the horses when they trampled him.

How ironic, Bailey thought, *He killed so many horses, then they killed him. Now that's justice.*

Bailey climbed back up the outcroppings and saw the lights were closer. He needed to get to town. Climbing down the same route through the rocks and brush they had come up, he reached his truck as the S.O.'s outfits were climbing up the road of the canyon. He turned his truck towards Rawlins and drove as fast as possible to the highway by Lamont. When he pulled onto the highway he pushed the pedal to the floor and hoped an animal didn't run across the road in front of him.

When Bailey reached town, he turned and drove to the house that he knew so well. He rang the doorbell, standing there with blood on his face and mud on his clothes.

Dennis Cummings answered the door in his robe and with a look of surprise, took Bailey's arm and led him into the living room.

"My God, Bailey, what's happened to you?" The concern in his voice sounded real. He looked at Bailey with a mask of emotion. His eyes seemed to look questionably into Bailey's. Dennis took fast, little steps to the glass hutch, opened the door, took out a glass and bottle and poured the glass half full. He brought it over to Bailey.

"Here, you look like you need this."

"I need to get Dana, Dennis. Where is she?" Bailey didn't take the offered glass. He saw the moving boxes stacked, the portraits gone from the wall and the oriental rugs rolled up.

"She's in the back, Bailey, sleeping for now. I gave her some sedatives to help her sleep." Cummings knocked the whisky down in one swallow and went back to the hutch and poured more into the glass. His back was to Calhoun.

"It's over, Dennis. I'm not quite sure of all the facts, but I know that you're behind this. I know about the refuge reverting back. There's enough on you now you'll go to prison for a long time. Calvin's dead. Streck and his two cronies are dead; Meade's dead."

Cummings froze for an instant. His arm dropped in front of him and he turned back to face Bailey, a chrome pistol in his hand.

"Bailey," he said with his soft, soothing voice. "If everyone is dead, then I can still make it. If I take care of you, then there will be nobody left to accuse me. Everyone knows I'm recovering from heart surgery. How could I have been involved?"

"Because you're burned, Dennis. There was a snitch in the mob at Vegas. He told how they had a guy on the payroll in the BLM Lease Department that had slipped them the bids on property and mining claims for years. Said they made a shit-pot load of money. He gave the FBI your name." Bailey shook his head. "Christ, I can't believe you did it. I thought I knew you."

"That shows you aren't very smart, Bailey. When I got transferred here, I did the same thing; just not as many opportunities, but I still made twice what I received in salary." He gestured with his arm to include the room.

"The paintings, oriental rugs, they were all originals. Worth a fortune and now on their way to my new home." He motioned with the pistol.

"Back up, Bailey."

Calhoun's eyes never left Dennis's face. He took a step back, dragging a leg, arms hanging down at his sides.

"Has it been worth it? All the killing? You know you'll be on the run now for the rest of your life." Bailey grimaced and put his hand on his leg.

"Of course it's worth it. But you're wrong as usual. I'll be living in a place no one will find me. No extradition if they do. A place where a little money buys anonymity."

Bailey held his leg and the look of defeat and resignation masked his face.

"I do like you and Dana, Bailey. I see you're hurt; it's time to get this unpleasantness over with. But I'm curious. How did you find out about the refuge? That impresses me."

"Dana did some research and found out about it reverting back if the horse population drops. I knew a count was coming, but I had no idea why." He clinched his teeth in obvious pain.

"I'll take that whiskey, Dennis."

"No, too late for a drink now, Bailey. I'm sorry."

"I should have known there would be some fucking, crooked politicians involved. I didn't know about you until tonight. A friend of mine in the Secret Service got the information from the feds and called me when I was on my way to the refuge."

"You knew about me and still went out to the refuge, leaving Dana here? Jesus Christ, Bailey. What the hell is the matter with you?" Cummings smirked, not looking like the kind grandfather anymore. He took another sip of the whiskey.

Bailey staggered forward a little. Haggard looking, head down, he seemed to have trouble catching his breath.

"Dennis, you shouldn't have fucked with Dana. That was your biggest mistake."

"Oh, really?" He said smugly. "Why?"

The last weeks of pent-up frustration were in the power of Bailey's fist as it flew out——hitting Cummings square in the breastbone. He hit him with all the strength he could muster. All of the rage built up in him was behind that punch.

Cummings flew back into the hutch. The crack of the bone bound with light wire, healing for only a month, sounded as if a shoring timber had split and snapped. The incision ruptured. His heart stopped from the shock of the blow. Cummings's shirt top started turning red from the blood that oozed out of his chest. Bailey had literally split his chest in half.

His eyes wide in disbelief, flowing silver hair disarrayed, he looked down to his chest then sank to the floor in a sitting position, his slippered feet sliding out in front of him, his back against the wall.

Bailey watched him die, then picked up the phone and called 911. Ignoring Cummings's body, Bailey stepped over it and went to the back bedroom where he found Dana unconscious from the drugs Cummings had given her. He gently picked her up from the bed, letting her legs drag on the floor.

"Walk, sweetheart. Come on, you can walk."

The sound of a siren could be heard as she placed one foot in front of her and staggered forward, Bailey holding her protectively and tight in his arms.

Epilogue

The sun burned the morning chill out of the air. Patches of green grass were starting to show over the prairie and small rivulets of water ran down the gullies as the remaining snow melted.

The stallion, tail held high, raced across the prairie, leading his herd west toward the foothills of Green Mountain.

STEPHEN PAUL has worked at an oil refinery, as a wrangler on a dude ranch, a firefighter for the Bureau of Land Management, and as a police officer. He presently lives with his wife, Judy, and their two mixed-breed pups, Callie and Barney, in Rawlins, Wyoming.

Stephen's short stories have received several awards and have appeared in Peeks and Valleys literary journal, WritersNet Anthologies, and Skyline Magazine. *Can Horses Cry?* is his first novel. He's currently working on a second novel about cattle genetics and murder, set in the resort town of Saratoga, Wyoming.

He encourages comments and can be contacted at bailey82301@yahoo.com

Printed in the United States
23051LVS00003B/286-312